The Carriage Driver^2

by

Michael Friedman

Mockingbird Books and Publishing

ISBN-10: 0-9860114-6-0
ISBN-13 978-0-9860114-6-7

Dedicated to

Katie C. Friedman

Introduction

I savored every word in every chapter of *The Carriage Driver* by Michael Friedman. These stories triggered my memories and experiences in the loss of those closest to me. While I gained powerful perspectives and even comfort from the original stories published in the Fall of 2015, I wanted more - much more...

My wish has turned into reality. *The Carriage* Driver^2 contains twenty-seven more stories with the Carriage Driver and his beloved Nuelle.

Some stories will be connected to each other, while all will deliver the same well - developed characters and life circumstances as found in the first edition. Even if this is your first exposure to the series, you will find yourself promptly immersed in stories rich with history, metaphor and depth.

Friedman seamlessly relays Captain Griffin Chaffrey's story with his companion, Nuelle, in the Civil War. We finally discover 'what makes the Carriage Driver tick' as he assists one of his men in finding the perfect haunt for him to rest in peace for eternity.

In another story, we learn of Griffin's decency in 'bending the rules' by allowing a father to give a last earthly gift to his daughter in the form of a dance - before starting the next journey.

Griffin reveals a distinctly tender side, as he checks with a young passenger: "Have you said your goodbyes? Did you remember your father and brothers and sisters?" In turn, this sweet lad, with innocent curiosity, melts a Ghastly Knight - traveling on a heavenly course.

Griffin is protective - a hero through the ages, assuring a young mother that her son will be safe, secure and loved by kind strangers, as she moves on from a life of battering and abuse.

Nuelle has grace and intuition - the best of partners with her faithful Carriage Driver. Together they remind us that everyone has a story - a past, a reason, a glimmer as to what kind of people they will become in the later years of life. Even in death, insights can be gained and forgiveness can occur from within.

In another installment, Friedman captures the brilliance of a madman - who would orchestrate songs of the universe throughout eternity.

In yet another, we see a compassionate Veterinarian surrounded by the animals he cared for - as he enjoys his story playing before him in the theater of life - finally assured of the powerful legacy he has left behind.

A homeless man never loses his decency, kindness and humanity through a life of cruelty. His next chapter found him to be the most heavenly of teachers.

The consummate chef reminds us that: "You get out of the pot what you put into it" as he continued his life's passion into the next dimension.

If such is the case, you are about to partake in a pot bursting with savory and well-spiced stories by Michael Friedman that will fill you with satisfaction, hope and wonder. Enjoy a copy for yourself and someone in your life who could benefit from this food for thought.

Maria Jordan, Author, Nurse, Teacher
Jeffersonville. PA

Preface

The Carriage Driver is your liaison to the heaven of your choosing. The ride is free; of course, you have paid in advance. Nuelle is his beautiful white mare; she gently guides the carriage through the streets of Boston. Neither the Carriage Driver nor Nuelle, suggest or offer your destination. That is up to you once you are invited up the step into the carriage. And there is no hurry in the decision. You are welcome to wait at the castle in the sky for as long as you like.

Captain Griffin Chaffey is, *The Carriage Driver*. When he and his men met death in a Civil War skirmish, he refused to go to his resting place until every man in his command found judgment. He found solace in this work and continued throughout the war carrying souls from both sides, as death has no politics.

After the war, Griffin returned to his home in Boston to continue his work. You will find here in these pages the stories of children, the homeless, and the one lost in his madness. Some stories glimpse into the battles to get the fare to heaven paid, the struggle with temptation. The Captain runs into a motley crew in a graveyard who wish to know why their names were not in the book.

These stories are to entertain, not to enlighten. They were written to awaken the imagination, not to preach or enforce established concepts. The Promised Land is just over the hill; glimpse inside the lives of those extended an invitation.

Enjoy the companionship between Captain Griffin and Nuelle as they share an apple together before each ride. Here there is no forbidden fruit. Find what you love and make it your heaven.

Table of Contents

The Carriage Driver[2] - Yumi's Flight

A black bird jumped along the picket fence outside Yumi's dirty window. A wren sat on the window rail and pecked at the glass. The room was quiet with death. Yumi's spirit had left her tall, slender body and stood watching in a corner. Her long departed sister walked into the room with a raven on her shoulder and a flight of sparrows circling.

Yumi's husband, Kuro, entered the room trailed by a deceit of lapwings. He picked up her wrist and felt for a pulse. When he found no pulse, he began searching through the drawers of the room looking for anything of value. When he stood to leave the room with what trinkets there were in his pockets, he scattered the sparrows as he walked right through the sister startling the raven and amusing Yumi.

The room was dark with flight and deceit. Yumi left her body and her visitors and walked out the front door into the Boston twilight. A delicate scent from the Charles River mesmerized Yumi and drew her in its direction. She stayed on Clarendon Ave. as the dome-shaped crowns of the yellow flowering, Golden rain trees teased her newly revitalized senses.

The Carriage Diver stood by Nuelle and brushed her coat as they waited on Clarendon Ave. It was not long before he saw Yumi approach as she looked this way and that.

Yumi stopped by the carriage and admired Nuelle's beauty. "Can you help me?" She asked.

The Carriage Driver tossed the brush he was using on to the front seat of the carriage. "I think I can. Do you know where you want to go?"

"I have an idea," she replied.

The Carriage Driver extended his hand to her, "Step inside."

"I am not sure you can take me where I want to go." Yumi was reluctant.

"Where do you want to go?"

Yumi sighed. "My mother read me a story once about a bamboo forest. At the center of the forest was a pond where all the beauty of the world began. Legend has it that many an artist died in their quest into the forest, as once they began their journey to bring beauty to the world, they were caught like flies on fly paper, unable to tear themselves free from the exquisite visions. Many years passed as beauty continued to be hidden from the world.

One day a blind man lead by a dog arrived at the village below the forest. In the pouch of this old artist were sheets of Washi paper. The villagers gathered. On them were paintings of orange Palomino Koi that looked big enough to ride and drawing after drawing of the bamboo plant. There were also watercolor paintings of butterflies of four shades of yellow that looked as if they would take flight from the delicate paper. The young artists were stunned by the beauty and vowed to enter the bamboo forest.

The old man told the tales of the first artist who perished in the forest. The old man sat on the ground with his dog at his side, picking at the rice from the bowl that was brought to him. Then he explained to the young artist of the village that if they entered the forest after dark, their lives and sight might be saved.

In the late afternoon a few of the braver of the young artists gathered their wooden boxes containing their watercolors and their paper. They sought out their mothers and asked for candles to carry. When darkness eased down from the sky the artists set off.

The artists quietly trekked to the pond and found spots to work. One sat near the pond cross-legged and then lit a small candle held in a cradle suspended above his eyes like a miners light. In the dark, the forest was spotted with the glow of these candles. Each artist's eyes could only see a halo of beauty and in this way, slivers of awe were created and brought out into the world.

During the day, the artist slept with blindfolds. These artists toiled at night, as they were desperate to bring the perfection of the bamboo's gentle leaf to the world. They came to believe the bamboo leaf generated souls."

She stopped and looked at the Carriage Driver. "Can you take me there?"

The Carriage Driver climbed up into the driver's spot and pulled a scroll from beneath his seat. He unrolled it and studied it for a long while. The Carriage Driver scrolled his finger back and forth across his map. His lips moved as he read some of the names. *Adra, Avalon, Camelot, Graceland, Jumanji, Narnia, Oz, and Wizarding World were marked and even Atlantis.** There were also castles, green pastures, galaxies, communes, and lakesides marked. He saw tropical Pacific islands, and mountain retreats, but no bamboo forest. He made a face and climbed down, "Your Bamboo Forest is not marked on my map." He paused, not having ever been asked to deliver any one someplace not on the map. "I can take you the rest of the way to the Charles River," he said trying to be helpful.

Yumi thought of long years with her cold husband who thought there was beauty in money. She thought of her sister entering her room with an invitation to reside in the land of the Ravens. Her mind drifted to the Wren tapping her window in an invitation to beyond tomorrow. She walked over and patted Nuelle on the shoulder. She straightened and turned toward the river.

"I want to spend my hereafter at the fountain of beauty," she said to Nuelle, who tossed her mane and swished her tail.

Her smile was the warmest the Carriage Driver ever saw. He watched in amazement as Yumi transformed into a blue crane and took two steps, spread her wings and flew towards the Charles River in search of the Bamboo Forest.

The Carriage Driver[2] - First-round draft

Joshua in Records was flipping through the last few pages of Edna's Life Book. He lifted the book and carried it over to Consul, where he expected quick approval and the *Emissary* stamp. Consul looked up when Joshua entered, it was a rare event. "What is it?"

"Take a quick look at this." Joshua handed the book to Consul.

Consul glanced at the last page with entries and noted there were just a few blank pages left. He flipped back and forth and read a few passages. He opened the book to the title page, lifted the *Emissary* stamp and stamped the book. He lifted the book and handed it back. He lifted a document and filled it out and stamped it approved.

Joshua returned to Records and sent copies of the stamped document to the heads of The Great Hall, The Saint's Delegation, The First Sanctuary Circle, and The Tribune of Solomon. Joshua felt satisfied though there was no hurry. A lot could happen while those last few pages in the life book were filled out.

A decade passed quickly; allowing little time for the counsel's to prepare their presentations.

Nuelle always enjoyed when the Carriage Driver climbed down and the two of them shared an apple. It usually meant the waiting for their fare was near an end and they could enjoy a journey to wherever they wished. This mild evening was no different. The glow from the street lamps cast a warm halo over the carriage, Nuelle, and the Carriage Driver.

The Carriage Driver gave a curious look in the direction of the person walking toward them. There was something stately about the figure. It was the figure of someone totally self-assured and radiant. Her clothing was plain, her eyes were not.

When she arrived, the Carriage Driver held out his hand to assist her inside. Nuelle swished her tail and tossed her mane.

"Am I in the right place?" She asked while admiring Nuelle's beauty.

"Yes, Ma'am, you picked a beautiful night for your journey. Just look at the stars out to welcome you." When she was seated, he said, "There is a blanket, near your feet, for your legs if you need it." He climbed aboard and gave Nuelle her rein.

Both Nuelle and the Carriage Driver were slightly excited by their passenger. They did not know why, there was just something about her. Nuelle headed toward the Commons because a festival was in progress and she felt the passenger would embrace the images and music. Her gate was slow through the park.

She reached the cobblestone road leading to the castle, which was the first stop for many passengers. The sound of Nuelle's hoofs and carriage wheels against the cobblestones showered the passenger with peace.

Edna gasped when the castle came into sight. In a short time, Nuelle reached the front of the castle, near the large wooden doors. There were a number of carriages waiting, from barouches to landaus. Some were elaborate and some were not. Nuelle pulled to a stop and the Carriage Driver climbed down and assisted Edna from the carriage. As she thanked the Carriage Driver, the doors opened and a tall, slim man wearing a tuxedo walked out to greet her.

Nuelle made a slow turn back towards home. The Carriage Driver waved to the other drivers and footman that were standing about.

The man in the tuxedo, took the cloak from Edna's shoulders and hung it near the hearth where a small fire was burning. He invited her to sit down. As he did a woman wearing white appeared and asked if she would like something to eat.

Edna acknowledged that she would and the young woman went through a door to the busy kitchen. In a moment, a bowl of Boston clam chowder, a side of fried clams, and a pint of ale were placed in front of her. The woman in white told her the main course would be served shortly; as there was a large party of people here this evening.

Music from a satin trumpet filtered through the air. The head of The Saint's Delegation came through the kitchen door carrying Edna's halibut with mushrooms. He set the plate down in front of her and took the seat opposite. The woman in white cleared the chowder bowl and brought two more glasses of ale.

He smiled, "Welcome, by the luck of the draw I won the first chance to present my case why you should join us at The Saint's Delegation. It is our joy to find those in the world today that have the makings of Saints. When we find them, we send, unknownst to them, emissaries that guide them to their calling. Those that have joined us are very satisfied with their choice."

Edna tried to look casual as she put a forkful of halibut in her mouth.

The sound of a woman clearing her throat was heard from the kitchen door. The man stood, "Promise you will think about it. You will travel the world."

The woman who so politely cleared her throat represented The Great Hall. She sat down in the vacated seat. "Hello, Edna. Is it true that you had a neighbor who moved in next door to you and was troublesome and impossible to get along with the whole time he was there, and when he got sick, you nursed him and took care of him until it was his time?" She paused and waited for an answer.

Edna put down her fork and took a sip of ale. "It is true. Deep, very deep down he was a good man." Edna smiled to herself, remembering the neighbor as all his prejudices melted away.

Her table guest took a sip of ale as well. "We are not as grand as The Saint's Delegation, but those working in the Great Hall are the finest artist to ever arrive here. We are working on a mosaic of the final battle between good and evil. We have become such a tight knit family and we would be honored to have you join us." She glanced over at the man in the doorway, knowing she had run a little over on her time to present. She reached over and patted Edna on the hand. Then stood and left.

A tall man, wearing a robe that dragged on the floor came over. He did not carry a glass of ale with him. "I head The Tribune of Solomon our task is to find ways to improve the quality of life of all the impoverished of the world. We don't hunt for Saints, although when we spot someone, we gladly refer them to the proper division." He paused and looked into Edna's face, but did not see the interest he had hoped to see. "It is not as glamorous of work, as is The Great Hall, but it is honorable work." He was finished and pushed his chair back. Standing, he said, "We are told the meek will inherit the earth. We were just not told when." He walked back to the kitchen.

The representative of The First Sanctuary Circle carried two cups of coffee over to the table and set them down. She took the empty seat. "You have now met some souls that hold very important roles here. Each group has an important function and as we have all taken the opportunity to look at your Life Book and come to the same conclusion. We all want you. The First Sanctuary Circle unlike the Tribune of

Solomon works to improve the hereafter. It seems that each generation arriving has modified their expectations and since we are 'the reward' we thought this should reflect that. We are not as warm as those working in The Great Hall. To tell the truth, I sometimes wish I would have chosen to be with those bohemians, gypsies, and hippies. There is always laughter from their quarters." She picked up her cup and took a sip.

Over by the kitchen door stood the other heads of the divisions. "You can take as long as you need to think about it. Or you can select now, there are carriages outside to take you to your new family."

Edna took a sip from her coffee. It was the best coffee, she ever tasted. "I have a question."

"Yes, what is it?" She was standing.

"Does God have a Dog Park?"

The Carriage Driver[2] - Sister Sarah's Secret

For those with vision, the neutral gray walls and oatmeal colored floor of Boston General did not hide the pockmarks left by every tear and drop of blood to hit the floor. Sister Sarah's sandals moved along the corridor towards the elevator doors that she viewed as the arteries that lead to the darkest recesses of pain and suffering.

When she reached the elevator, the doors slid open with an ominous quiet. She clutched her rosary and stepped inside, then she was whisked off to the top floor. When the door opened, she looked passed the calm, into the hideousness and helplessness. She turned to her right and marched defiantly towards eight-year-old Constance's room.

Constance lay in her bed. She wore a yellow turban on her head for both warmth and to hide the loss of her hair. She smiled when Sister Sarah entered. Sarah was in a hurry this morning. She moved close to the bed. She gently placed her thumb on Constance's right eyelid and leaned over and kissed her left eyelid. Healing energy flowed through Constance forcing diseased cells from the child's body, permeating Sarah's lips and invading her body. In a moment Sarah stood, touched Constance on the forehead. The child slept.

Sarah looked at her notes. She walked toward the doorway, back to the elevator. The corridors, infested with the pains of humanity guided her. At the doorway of Gregory, a middle-aged man she stepped inside. His hands were crippled with arthritis and he wore his pain like a crown for all to see. She knelt and prayed, running her rosary through her youthful fingers. When she was finished, she stood, put her index finger on his right eyelid and gently placed her lips on his left eyelid. Again the pulses of energy raced through the man. His crippled hands unfolded, the inflammation eased from him into Sister Sarah.

When she stood, she concealed her own hands beneath the sleeves of her frock and made her way slowly, without vigor to the next on her list. Mark, who was twenty, had a stroke while playing a Saturday baseball game. His stroke was caused by too much sun and not enough water. Sarah found him beautiful and though there were younger people on her list, she tried to share her secret equally.

Mark sat in a wheelchair staring out the window. Sister Sarah lifted a towel and dabbed the drool at the sides of his mouth. He smiled at the kindness. She stooped down and touched his eyelid with her middle finger and put her lips to his other eyelid. His constricted arteries opened as her own closed. She moved her mouth and kissed his forehead. A sigh escaped his lips.

Sarah made it to the doorway. Her right side slumped. Her sandals slowly scraped along the floor of the corridor. The rosary swayed along gripped by the hand hidden by her sleeve. She leaned against the wall for a moment and then forced herself upright and towards Carol's room.

There were two nurses with Carol when Sarah arrived. Sarah took the empty chair and bowed her head in prayer until the nurses completed their duties.

"Did you bring it?" Carol asked once the nurses left.

"Yes, I brought it. Are you ready?" Sarah replied.

Carol sat up the best she could. She had a rare cancer of the eyes. Usually, adults were diagnosed with the disease, but it had found its way to this child.

"Are you ready?" Sarah asked again. She loved to see Carol's smile. Without waiting for a response, she touched her ring finger to Carol's right eye and her lips to her left eye. In a moment, Sarah's eyes only saw blurry gray and she stood and followed the light toward the door with Carol's laughter and glee ringing in her ears.

Sarah now used the wall as her guide. She reached the room of a writer with a pulmonary embolism. He often spoke with Sarah as she made her rounds.

As she stepped inside, he said, "Sarah, you must sit down. You must be having a terrible day."

"On the contrary, I am having the most extraordinary day." She smiled at the thought. The pain in her hands wracked through her. Her eyes hurt, her face was dull.

"John, I never told you, but…," she stopped. She moved towards the bed and put her pinky on his eyelid. He felt the surge of energy and started to speak. She stopped him by placing a disfigured finger against his eye. She then, doing everything she could to keep her balance, leaned over and placed her lips on his other eye.

"There, that wasn't so bad. Right?" She had trouble shuffling away from the bed and out the door.

John took a deep breath, wondering what just happened and how it was that he could take a deep breath.

Using the wall as support, Sister Sarah made her way, back to the elevator, back to the artery that would allow her to escape. On the ground floor, she crept toward the front exit and down the steps.

Through pain and hardship, she pushed forward.

Nuelle swished her white tail and her mane at Sister Sarah's approach. The Carriage Driver watched as this wreck of a figure staggered towards them, rosary beads in hand. Her shoulders were slumped, hands crippled, breathing arrested, and insides infested. She made it to the curb and fell to the ground dead.

Slowly, the Carriage Driver climbed down and knelt by her side. In a moment, he lifted her, stepping up into the carriage and placed her on the leather seat. When he returned to his seat, he turned and asked Sarah if she were comfortable. The young, healthy woman sitting in the back, smiled a blissful smile.

Nuelle pulled the carriage onto the street, toward the kingdom. She walked at a leisurely pace. She walked past the castle. Wide gates swung open and once through a green pasture Nuelle stopped at a glade.

Sister Sarah climbed down, she stepped toward the drive and whispered, "Wait for me. I will only be a moment or two."

The Carriage Driver climbed down and walked toward Nuelle. He pulled an apple from his pocket and cut it into quarters. Two pieces he ate and two he fed to Nuelle. He patted her shoulder as he watched Sister Sarah make her way through acres of kneeling nuns. Alongside the nuns were kneeling priests, pastors, deacons, bishops, cardinals, abbots, and priors.

Sarah watched her step carefully. She made her way to her Father's feet. Upon reaching Him, she knelt and grabbed the hem of his garment.

"Sarah, what am I going to do with you?" He asked. "I have sent you to save souls." He paused and looked out over the thousands, who through the ages served his word. He reached down and touched Sister Sarah on the head, indicating she should stand. He smiled at her, "To save souls, not lives."

"Yes, my Lord." She turned with her rosary in her young, nimble hands and walked back through the acres of kneeling believers.

Sister Sarah took her Lord's smile as consent. She reached the Carriage Driver. "Take me back. There is work to be done."

The Carriage Driver climbed down and extended his hand to young Sarah. Once she was settled in the back, Nuelle made a full turn and made her way back towards the gates.

Sister Sarah's secret was safe with the Carriage Driver and Nuelle.

The Carriage Driver[2] - Sister Sarah's Miracle

It had been years since the miracle but Carol could never forget it. A rare cancer had been attacking her eyes. She was told that she would first lose her sight and there was not much medically that could be done to save it. The miracle happened on the fourth floor of Mass General Hospital.

Years later she would come to find out that hers was one of five miracles to happen that day. As a girl of eight, she was innocent as to the workings of the world. When a Sister from the church began to visit her, she was grateful for the company but held little understanding.

One evening, late after the nurses had finished their rounds, the Sister entered her room and sat and held her right hand. In the Sister's her left-hand rosary beads passed through her fingers as prayers were released.

Sister Sarah squeezed Carol's hand. "I know the doctors have told you there is no hope. I want to assure you that there is hope. You have to believe. The universe is full of things that mankind cannot explain." The Sister leaned back in her chair as she looked into this face of innocence. She felt such goodness in the presence of Carol.

"Do you believe in miracles?" Carol asked. Her sight had begun to go and her image of the Sister was not clear.

Sarah leaned forward as if to share a secret. "I not only believe in miracles, but I am also determined to bring you one."

"Oh, you mean you can just go out and find a miracle?" Carol leaned her weary head on the pillow and smiled at the thought.

Sarah stood and squeezed Carol on the shoulder. "I am going to start working on that right now. See you soon." She left to see a patient on the third floor.

Days went by and Carol prayed for her miracle and waited to see the Sister again. In those quiet hours after midnight when she could not sleep, she felt doubt. She just remembered she had to believe.

The night of the miracle was so clear in her mind. Sister Sarah entered her room and sat and waited for two nurses to finish checking the monitors. The lights were dimmed. Sister Sarah first held her hand and prayed using her rosary. When it was quiet, Sister Sarah leaned over and touched her eye with the tip of one finger and kissed her other eyelid.

The pressure in her head, which had hurt for months was gone. The light was dim, but she made out an aura of Sister Sarah as she stood. Then Sister Sarah put her arm out and felt her way along the bed towards the door.

Carol lay there. Her head had cleared and tears were running down her cheeks hitting the pillow. That was the last time she was ever in her presence.

There was such a buzz of excitement at the hospital in the morning. Everyone person in the building was talking about the miracles of the evening before. The majority were talking about Carol and her story that a miracle was delivered by a Sister of the cloth.

After several examinations and a few days of observation, the doctors released Carol to her anxious and thankful parents. They returned to their normal life.

When Carol was old enough to work, she began saving money. She set herself a goal and felt nothing could stop her. After all, she was leading a life that had been blessed. The years passed and finally she had money enough to open a modest florist shop near Mass General. Her life was returned to her there, and she felt a bond.

Carol flourished for years. In the florist trade, she developed a reputation for ingenuity and flair. An unspoken motto was to bring as much pizzazz into the lives of the patients who found themselves confined behind the walls of Mass General. She also developed some of the most colorful floral arrangements in the trade.

Her bouquets might consist of English violet and Hyacinths mingled with Mock-orange with an added slice of redwood bark as the blue and white contrast was a favorite. In her garden, she grew her own Damask rose and could never get enough. The light-red Damask rose and pink peony again with Mock-orange or Baby's breath was popular. She also offered bouquets of jasmine and carnations.

Carol continued for many years. Her shoulders began to stoop and her back ached. At long last she sold her business and retired to her garden. She spent her days with her Damask roses and her flower beds and she had begun waiting for her time.

The Carriage Driver rose from sleep early on a warm spring night. He dressed slowly and then went and fed Nuelle in her stable. He cleaned the carriage and polished the lanterns on each side of the front seat.

He brushed Nuelle and got her prepared for the day's journey.

Carol's spirit rose from the tired body and dressed in a soft flowing gown. She admired the return of her youthful figure and then walked out into her pleasant garden. She clipped the prettiest Damask rose and carried it with her.

The Carriage Driver went to the location in his book. It was a florist shop near Mass General. He climbed down and waited.

While waiting, he took the opportunity to share an apple with Nuelle. As he stood talking to Nuelle, he noticed her tail swish and she tossed her mane. He glanced up and saw a woman whose eyes sparkled walking in his direction.

He stood by the side of the carriage waiting for her to reach them. She paused and peered inside the window of the florist shop which once belonged to her. She then turned and walked toward the carriage.

Once she was inside and settled the Carriage Driver climbed up to his seat. "There is a blanket near your feet if you are at all cold." He paused, "That is a beautiful rose you are carrying."

Nuelle pulled away from the curb. There was no hurry in her step. In was a fine Boston morning.

Carol sat back in her seat and smiled. "As a child, I was blessed. I spent my life trying to repay that kindness. For years, I experimented with the mixture of flowers, for many reasons. But the main thing that stood out in my mind. How do I say it? The night of my blessing, my sight was returned, but also, there was a scent of heaven."

The Carriage Driver[2] - The Treasure Hunter

Most of the unemployed men in the neighborhood stopped in for coffee at the Pair a Dice Café a local coffee house. There was much talk between them as to how to generate income. Today Ralph came in with an old 'Western' magazine. The cover showed an old wooden chest with strong metal hinges. Gold coins overflowed the chest and lay about. A rattlesnake curled himself about a nearby skull.

"Look here," he began. "This here is a real treasure. The story claims an Army stage was carrying confiscated confederate gold when it was attacked by highwaymen. The highwaymen were hunted down, but were killed in the taking. The treasure is within twenty miles of where it was stolen, 'cause that's where the bandits were killed and the treasure has never been found."

Barry piped up."So why ain't no one found it? I mean if you think it is so easy." He took a sip of his cold coffee.

"They ain't looked hard enough." Ralph fired back.

Glen was more level headed. "Ralph you got a wife and kids. You can't just wander off looking for no treasure, that likely ain't there anyway. They are taking some men part time over on pier 13. It pays coffee money if nothing else. I am going over there this morning. Maybe I can keep the lights on."

Ralph flipped the pages of the magazine. The magazine was old and worn, the cover frayed. His imagination ran wild as he could feel the cold gold coins clutched between his fingers. His eyes glazed over. The fever took him. "I'm going to hunt it down. You go make pocket money on the pier." He got up and left the café.

Ralph knew he would catch hell from his wife. He waited down the street from his place and when he saw her leave for work went and gathered up a duffle bag with some meager belongings and headed toward the coast.

Two days later, Ralph has hunting along a rugged stretch of shoreline when some rocks tumbled away and he found himself at the mouth of a cave. It was one of those gray pounding days along the Atlantic. The winds howled and fury stirred the clouds. The gods were restless.

The knocking at the door pulled Claire back from sleep. She had fallen asleep sitting up in the living room chair. She shook her head and heard the knocking again. She stood and walked to the door.

Barry stood there. "Is Ralph in, I haven't seen him in two or three days now?" He stood there waiting.

"When you see that big S.O.B you tell him for me that he thinks he can go and leave for days at a time and then come crawling back here that he has another thing coming." She looked at Barry. "When is the last time you saw him? The kid is driving me crazy with worry."

Barry looked sheepish he cleared his throat. "We were having a coffee at Pair of Dice Café and he had this old magazine said there was a treasure hidden along the coast. He was guessing the only place that it could be was along Devil's Ridge otherwise they'd a found it by now."

"You're supposed to be his friend. You let him go exploring that cliffside area?" There was disgust on her face. "What's wrong with you men?" Her daughter Crystal walked into the room to see what was happening. Claire found a smile and put it on her face. "Thank you, Barry," she said while closing the door.

Claire turned to her daughter and picked her up. "Should I make us something to eat?" A real smile appeared as she looked into her daughter's eyes. "Are you hungry?" Claire concealed her concerns.

After dinner, Claire called her sister to see if she would watch Crystal for a couple of days. She packed an overnight bag for her daughter and brought her to her favorite aunts. She returned home. She dug through her closet and found some heavy dungarees a heavy shirt and ankle high boots and rain hat and went to the car. She made her way to Devil's Ridge.

The coastal waters pounded the shore. The sky was angered by her presence. "RALPH," she called. "RALPH!!" Claire walked along the lower edges of the cliffside until she found a place to begin her climb. The jagged edges of the rocks pressed hard against her as she began her ascent. A lot sooner than she thought the pain of exertion set in. Yet she climbed all the while calling Ralph's name.

The already dark sky became darker and the rains came hard. The heavy dungarees soaked up the rain and soon Claire was soaked through to the skin. The extra weight was oppressive and she made her way to a narrow ledge and lay there shivering with cold and anger. She closed her eyes tight against the flash of the lightning; then opened them to the sound of the Siren's song.

The Carriage Driver gently puts the harness over Nuelle's neck. This Atlantic storm was no place for man or beast. He finished the rigging. He found the heaviest blanket to use as a shield for Nuelle from the rain. He found his hat and tugged the heavy scarf around his neck and tucked the ends in his coat. The two stepped out together into harsh nature's wrath.

Nuelle lead them to their destination. The Carriage Driver knowing that there had never been a mistake regarding the location was confused at where they were. He climbed down and walked up to Nuelle. They exchanged glances as water poured along the lines of their faces. "Where is our fare?" The Carriage Driver looked around. "Wait here," he patted Nuelle and checked her blanket.

He made his way to the shore. He made his way to the edge of the cliff and started to climb. The jagged rocks grated like files against his knees and elbow. The icy rain stuck his hands like stinging whips. He found Claire lying on the narrow ledge. He slipped off the belt of his jacket and closed the heavy clasp. He slipped the belt over her head and under her arms. He then looped the belt over his head, pulling her close to his body and made his way back down the cliffside to the icy water.

He made his way back up to Nuelle.

Nuelle tossed her mane and swished her tail. The Carriage Driver sat Claire on the step of the Carriage.

Claire took a deep breath and raised her head. Seeing The Carriage Driver she found a smile and brought it to her face. "The Sirens told me you would be coming for me." She stood and seeing Nuelle rushed to her. "I am so sorry to bring you out in this." She drew her fingers along Nuelle's wet mane. "Oh, girl, I never thought I'd see anything as beautiful as you." She kissed Nuelle's cheek. To The Carriage Driver, she said, "Where is Ralph?"

"Ralph?"

"Yes, my husband. I was looking for him. I am sure he is here close by."

The Carriage Driver climbed up to his seat. He pulled a book from beneath the seat and looked at today's entry. "I don't show an entry for Ralph. I'm sorry." He climbed back down from the seat. "Would you like to climb up into the carriage? There is a blanket on the floor you can use for warmth."

The rain continued to strike the two. The Carriage Driver offered his hand.

"He was looking for treasure. The old fool."

"Seems he had all the treasure he needed."

She took his hand and climbed into the carriage. The icy rain stopped striking her.

Nuelle led the way to Claire's new journey.

The Carriage Driver[2] - Theater Life

Mary O'Donoghue ran out the front doors of Boston General wearing only a hospital gown. She spotted a carriage beneath the glow of the lamplight and headed towards it. Nuelle swished her mane and waved her tail.

The Carriage Driver climbed down and watched with interest the woman running at a sprint towards him. He could not recall a brighter smile. He tipped his hat back and waited.

When she reached him, she came to a stop and bent over with her hands on her knees. Breathing hard, she said, "I couldn't wait to get out of there. I was there for so long."

The Carriage Driver smiled at her and extended his hand to steady her as she climbed into the back. "There is a blanket there. Pull it around you if you are cold."

Mary reached for the blanket and draped it over her legs as Nuelle pulled the carriage from the curb. The Carriage Driver was mildly amused as Nuelle seemed to prance this evening. She leaned forward, "I worked in the same office my whole career. Of course, the name on the building kept changing. I think it was Southwest Bell Corp. when I got hired. Then that was modernized to SBC Communication and then AT&T was the name on the pay stub. But my job never changed, just the name on the building." She looked at her young hands and smiled. "I felt invisible the whole time."

Nuelle headed toward Massachusetts Ave toward Tremont Street. The night was balmy and energy pulsed from the Carriage Driver's passenger. The carriage practically glowed as it pulled down an alley to an open stage door.

Mary gazed at the street side of the alley. The sidewalk reflected the many colors from the marquees and billboards. The smell of coffee and the sounds from a bistro drifted towards them. The stage door swung open and a young man hurried to the side of the carriage. "Come on. We don't want to be late." He held out his hand as Mary stood and leaned over and kissed the Carriage Driver on the cheek. Then she climbed down and ran to Nuelle and kissed her cheek also.

The young man held his hand out and Mary took it as they rushed to the stage door. He pulled her along and let her hand go in front of racks of costumes. She looked this way and that and reached for a white gown. The young man untied the two knots holding the hospital gown and Mary let it drop to the floor.

"Hold up your arms," the young man said, as he dropped the gown over her head and zipped it. "Wait, I'll get the slippers." In a moment, she was wearing silver slippers and he was adjusting her sparkly tiara. He guided her to the left side of the stage and whispered, "When he reaches out his right arm you enter."

The handsome dark haired man on stage was dressed in cavalry attire, black pants with gold stripes and red jacket with golden epaulets and also a gold sash. He had just defeated a man in a sword duel. He turned and raised his right arm, and Mary walked out on stage as he began to sing in a baritone voice.

Mary entered the stage to applause as he sang. She looked out past the stage lights, her heart was racing and adrenaline was rushing through her. In a moment, to her surprise, she was also singing. In an hour, she found herself center stage, taking a bow, to a standing, applauding audience, with the handsome young man by her side.

As the curtain lowered, there was a great rush of excitement as the cast and crew rushed off stage. The crew was changing sets and the cast hurried here and there for costume changes. Mary again found the young man by her side as she stood in front of the racks of clothing from all time periods. He reached over and unfastened the zipper and she stepped out of the gown. The man frowned for a second, "Come with me." He led her to a door that to her surprise had her name on it and a star. They walked in. He raised his arm and pointed up and down at her. "There are some garments in those drawers that you might put on."

In a moment, Mary and the young man were back making a choice about what to wear. She selected a calf length western skirt and pulled it on. She also grabbed a snap button blouse from the clothing rack. He went and found a pair of cowgirl boots and white Stetson hat and helped her with the adjustments. He thought she looked stunning.

He led her to the side of the stage and, this time, a tall, handsome, blonde haired young man in western garb and carrying a guitar stood there. They entered the stage together and before long everyone on stage was singing and everyone in the audience's lips moved as they followed along.

A man in overalls was out walking along the catwalk adjusting the letters M.A.R.Y. O.'. D.O.N.O.G.H.U.E. along the lighted marquee. He was sure this was going to be a long run. He made sure all the lights were shining.

On stage, a cleverly lit spotlight casts a full moon above the handsome young cowboy as he sang a love song to Mary, who sat by the campfire. Mary finally was the star of her own show.

Nuelle was enjoying the serenading coming from the theater and was reluctant to go. The Carriage Diver pulled an apple from his pocket and cut it into quarters. He fed two to Nuelle and ate two. He sighed, and climbed back on board. At the touch of the reins, Nuelle pulled the carriage toward the street that was glistening with lights and laughter. She stepped high along the boulevard feeling quite full of the joys of life. The Carriage Driver let Nuelle set the pace. The night was radiant, filled with people enjoying the best life had to offer. The cafes and restaurants were busy and people stood in line waiting their chance to be in the presence of Mary O'Donoghue.

After the second performance, Mary found herself walking down the street with the tall blonde man on one arm and the dark haired beauty on the other arm. She was taking in all the sights and sounds. She ran through all the costumes she could remember on those racks. It occurred to her that the costume she chose set the tone of the play she was to perform in next. The thought amused her and she thought she was going to have a lot of fun. To those passing by it seemed as Mary pranced down this street of dreams.

The Carriage Driver[2] - The King of Quiet Hearts

The doors of L'Osteria on Salem Street were closed today. The restaurant was booked for the wedding reception by the family of Patty, a longtime waitress there. The community loved her for her style and charm. Patty was quick with the wine and slow with the check. Her magnetism and chatter could ignite a conversation at the sourest of tables. Her big day had finally arrived.

On this day-of-days Patty was feeling uneasy. Her bridesmaids, on the way to the Church of the Covenant, assured her that was natural. They all laughed and the unmarried bridesmaids tucked their envy aside.

Henry, the groom, paced, in a side room of the church; his friends that had agreed to rent tuxedos and stand for him were there for him while laughing and making jokes about hopping in their jeeps and heading for Mexico.

When the guests were finally seated and the priest took his place, the music began. The bride stood at the end of the aisle with her father at her side. On cue, they started walking toward the altar. Her handsome groom watched their every careful step. Patty had joked more than once that one wrong step and she would be standing in a room filled with family and friends wearing only lace underwear with her dress bunched around her ankles.

The thought that he looked pale came into the groom's head just as Patty clutched her father's arm tightly. His legs gave way and he crumpled to the ground. She knelt by him and the groom rushed to her as family and friends stood and leaned toward the disaster unfolding before them.

She held him with tears in her eyes. Nuelle stopped the carriage outside the church. It was a beautiful day with just the slightest breeze carrying fresh cleansing Atlantic air. The

Carriage Driver climbed down, he took an apple from his pocket and cut it into four pieces.

Henry helped Patty to her feet. Time moved slowly, she seemed to be able to see every movement in the church. With her head turned toward the entrance, she saw her father walk out into the sunlight. Her head was spinning and she was losing her color.

Patty rushed toward the door, leaving Henry kneeling by her father. One of the bridesmaids followed after Patty.

Her father, Kimble stood by the carriage. "What is going on?" he asked.

The Carriage Driver fed two pieces of apple to Nuelle. "Sir, it is your time."

"Nonsense, can't you see where we are? There must be some mistake." The look of concern and consternation fought for control of his face.

The Carriage Driver handed Kimble the two extra pieces of apple. Kimble then walked over and fed them to Nuelle.

The Carriage Driver lifted his hat, scratched his head and returned the hat to its location. He spotted Patty standing in the doorway and a redheaded bridesmaid by her side. "Mistake sir, we are not known for mistakes." He looked at the bride. He walked over and lifted Nuelle's front right foot and glanced at Kimble. "Sorry, sir, there is going to be a slight delay."

Gratitude won the contest for control of Kimble's face. "Sir, please join us inside."

Kimble, Patty, and the Carriage Driver walked back inside the church. The Carriage Driver took a seat in the back row. He put his hat in his lap.

Kimble opened his eyes and let out an uncomfortable laugh. Henry helped him to his feet. "Sorry folks. Sorry. I am so nervous today." He raised his voice and gave a hollow laugh.

Patty took his arm - her heart was pounding so loudly she thought the nearest guests might be able to hear it. Her head turned as far as it could to see The Carriage Driver seated in the back row. Confusion reigned. Henry resumed his place and the music restarted.

It was a beautiful ceremony. As the ritual came to an end, The Carriage Driver put his hat back on, ducked out and walked to the carriage. Nuelle waited patiently. "Take me to the park," he called to Nuelle. "I want to sense the beauty of life." The wheels clicked and clattered against the pavement. Nuelle swished her tail and tossed her mane. Her pace was slow and her attitude nonjudgmental. When done and the new couple was announced as bride and groom they left the church and their guest flowed towards the restaurant.

It is not often that you walk into a room bursting with joy. But that is what the guests were greeted with as they entered L'Osteria. The music was played at just the right level. The guests were served quickly once seated. The chicken stuffed with shrimp and cheese was gobbled up as was the veal braccioletttine. The red wine poured from gallon bottles in the kitchen and a glass was never empty for long.

The best man got to his feet and made his toast that made the groom weep, all thoughts of Mexico gone now. Then the father-daughter dance was announced.

Kimble held his daughter and they turned slowly to the music. "I am so proud of you. This has been the best night of my life. Seeing you so happy and knowing you found a man that will take care of you means the world to me. He is one lucky man to have earned your love."

"I love you, Dad," Patty told him.

"I know you have always thought me too quiet. But my heart has always been at peace. You will see, sometimes it is time for loud and boastful and other times reflection can be its own reward."

Patty squeezed her father's hand and smiled as the music stopped.

In a very few moments the bride and groom made their way to the waiting limousine that would take them to the airport. Their honeymoon waited.

The evening continued on. Wedding party members and guests slowly finished their wine and began to filter out into the night. The stars sparkled and the gaslights along the boulevard gave the scene a fairytale essence as the music seemed to trail them along the street. Several of the guests thought they heard the sound of carriage wheels moving slowly along the cobblestoned street as they made their way to waiting cabs.

Kimble leaned against the bar, a glass with ice and a generous portion of bourbon in his hand. The feeling of pride swirled through him. The Carriage Driver walked into the front door and joined Kimble at the bar. Kimble reached behind the bar for a glass and poured three fingers into the glass.

The Carriage Driver lifted his glass and said, "To the King of Quiet Hearts," and drank down his elixir. As the two walked toward the front door, Kimble's legs gave way beneath him.

Kimble stood in the doorway and watched as the redheaded bridesmaid and her date for the evening rushed to his side - a look of panic on her face. They were the last two guests in the restaurant. She rushed around looking for her purse. Once found, she retrieved her phone and dialed.

"911 Operator. What is your emergency?"

The Carriage Driver[2] - Philharmonic Voyager

Ben, in his madness, stood by the St. Charles River waving his arms and listening to an orchestrated delivery of the song of the universe. The planets called to him; there was an allure to the majesty of their sounds. Thunder bellowed from the brass section and lightning clapped the percussions. A gentle wind whipped through the River birch and silver bells which added a woodwind accompaniment. The light string sounds of the viola and violins came from water gliding along the reeds near the bank of the river.

Music pulsed through him. His trembling hands waved to the right to raise the thunder and waved down low to slow the tempo. The baton extended directly to the heavens brought lightning on cue, directed by God. He nodded to the reeds to send them into the score and waved one arm in each direction to signal the rustle of rushes.

Inside his rumpled grayish suit sweat dripped down his sides. The white hair bristled above his eyes. And those music-filled blazing blue eyes pierced into the intimacy of space. He was engulfed in a symphonic, prismatic, stereographic rapture that rumbled through his electrified heart.

A long-haired young man by himself lay down on his side and propped up his head with his hand and watched. Then a young woman with two small girls stopped, sat and waited. After a moment, another woman with a young daughter in tow followed suit. The notes from the movement on the grassy knoll added to the ensemble. The usually unnoticed section of lawn became a showground.

A family of wood thrush found seats in a birch, and when the baton waved in their direction, they articulated the tempo. With waving reeds, rustling rushes, clapping lightning, trembling thunder; Ben poured his very last heartbeat into the concert that had been his life. As dusk began pulling his curtain closed, Ben heard the sound of metal rimmed wheels along a cobblestone road accompanied by beckoning hoof beats.

Ben walked through the grass towards the sound of the wheels. He thought he recognized the young beauty with two daughters as his first wife from long ago. He stopped and gave the three of them hugs and one last smile. The second mother and child looked familiar also. He knelt and gave the child with blazing blue eyes an embrace, he hoped she would remember for all her days. He paused at the smiling young man who was now standing and wondered what had become of him. Nuelle heard the youngest girl ask her mother, "Why was that man waving his arms in the wind?"

As Ben moved away from the shoreline, he looked back over his shoulder. They were all watching him. The women had aged, and their daughters had grown into women. Only the young man remained young, and he was waving. The wood thrush flew away, and the thunder quieted. Now the trees were just trees.

Nuelle obediently pulled the carriage near. Nuelle felt immense loss tonight: as the sky had become quiet. The movement of the river went unnoticed as its orchestra case closed and floated towards the sea along the empty bank.

Ben began to rush. As his arms swung tree limbs rattled maracas and their leaves, their castanets; the treschyotka pursued his footsteps. He raised his hands to his face and cymbals crashed. He came to a stop at the carriage and walked over to Nuelle. He put his ear to her side and listened to her heart roar like a thundering herd of wild horses.

The Carriage Driver climbed down. He took an apple from his pocket and quartered it. He fed two pieces to Nuelle and ate the others. Nuelle warmed by the attention of Ben and her love of The Carriage Driver.

"Were you sent for me?" Ben asked with sparkling eyes.

"You are in the book," he smiled. "The notation by your name is unusual. It says you can be picked up any time of your choosing. I have been driving now for some time, and I never saw a notation like that."

The Carriage Driver's words poured over him like a piano concerto. Each and every syllable was a note carrying a wave of warmth. Ben imagined what a father's embrace would be like as he let the words sweep over him. Standing this near to The Carriage Driver and Nuelle brought almost unbearable joy.

The Carriage Driver walked over in front of Nuelle and took her face in his hands. "Are you ready for this," he asked.

Nuelle swished her long white tail and tossed her mane. He took a deep breath, and walked over and extended his hand to Ben. He said, "If you care to step inside."

The earth had turned a full rotation before the hand was accepted and Ben took that step.

A young man with long brown hair sat in the back of the carriage. His pant legs were flared at the end. His shirt was unbuttoned halfway, showing his tanned chest. But most notable were his blue lagoon eyes. His gaze took in everything. "Say something," said the voice from the back seat.

"You will find that for this journey, every utterance will not be melodious. Every hoof step will not be the striking of the Taiko drums. You will be able to hear the grass talking if you wish, and rays of sunshine will not echo through you. Nuelle will avoid going through the chaos of the city. Do you know where you want to go?"

"I haven't given this any thought. Is there time to tell me all the choices? Just how does this work?"

"We can try to give you the time you need. We do have other guests." The Carriage Driver thought a moment and then gave Nuelle rein to stop. He reached under his seat and finding the map handed it back to Ben.

Nuelle began the journey again as Ben studied the map. "I suppose Woodstock is out of the question?" Ben flashed a smile.

"A man with your sensitive ears might want to carefully consider where he spends the next leg of the journey."

"You are right. That might not be wise. Did you say next leg? How many legs to the voyage are there?" Ben leaned forward still holding the map.

"For each person that begins their journey with us, there are different legs. Some people are spiders; some are centipedes. Many travelers go in different directions. Very few journeys ever end."

With this new information, Ben sat back and became quiet as he looked at the map and enjoyed the tour of the Commons that Nuelle was taking. He wondered where this magnificent white beast would take him if he did not give a destination. Ben looked up, "So if I tire of a place I will be able to move on? That is what I understood you to say."

"Yes, very few end their journey in one place. Many find companions that they travel time with."

Ben smiled again, "Sounds like there should be guides."

The Carriage Driver laughed. He was the first guide on Ben's journey. He resumed silence.

Ben looked at the map. He spotted something in the upper left corner. He tapped his finger a couple of times while thinking. "Take me here." He leaned forward and pointed to a place on the map called the *Whispering Tunnels*.

The Carriage Driver knew, Nuelle was already on her way.

The Carriage Driver[2] - Christopher Conant

Christopher Conant in his kitchen at the Oyster House added cayenne pepper to the bouillabaisse, dipped a wooden spoon and brought the broth to his lips. He let out a sigh, glanced at the impatient waitress and picked up the ladle. He filled waiting bowls with generous portions of broth with rockfish, red Rascasse, and turbot. He set the ladle down. He grabbed a skimmer and plunged it into another pot with velvet crabs, sea urchins, and mussels and dropped his catch into each bowl.

The waitress hauled bowls onto her tray, came about and headed for port. Chef Conant watched her go. As she went, she leaned to starboard from the weight of the tray. He grabbed a handful of *scallions* and with practiced precision cut them into quarter-inch pieces dropping them into his pot.

He grabbed two cleaned perch, opened them and stuffed them with shrimp, placing them in a pan and brushed the surface with lemon butter. In a moment, they were on the grill. In a matter of minutes, they would be joined by pearl onions in white sauce and garlic mashed potatoes, served *à la Florentine.*

He pulled the cork from his bottle of Martin Codax and filled his wine glass. He lifted the glass, looked toward heaven and said, "You have taken away the women and the good looks, but not the wine." He took a drink, laughed and pulled the pan from the grill. He spread the baby leaf spinach, drizzled the white sauce with pearl onion over them and placed the stuffed perch on top. He scooped the garlic mashed potatoes onto the plate and watched as in sailed the waitress. His voyage had taken years, but he had discovered his happiness. In his empty kitchen, under his breath, he mouthed the Elton John song 'Tiny Dancer' and did mock dance steps.

The Carriage Driver stood by Nuelle and said, 'It's time." She was not happy about this assignment. She sensed that so much good was leaving. At a slow gait, she headed to Union Street for the appointment scheduled in the book on the day Christopher was born.

Midnight arrived, in the dining room, the last of the guests were paying their bills and gathering their coats. The piano player closed the fallboard. The busboys cleared. In the back, Christopher Conant let the cleaning crew in the back door and said good night as he left.

The Carriage Driver fed Nuelle two quarters of an apple. He watched as Christopher, shoulders stooped over in the cold, came closer. When he began to pass, the Carriage Driver cleared his throat, "Christopher," he called.

Chef Conant looked up from his thoughts, on how to improve his soubise, and seeing The Carriage Driver and Nuelle showered in the glow of two gas lamps stopped. This heavyset man straightened and took a step forward. "What is it?"

Nuelle swished her tail and shook her long white mane. The Carriage Driver said, "We have been sent for you. If you'd care to step into the carriage, we will take you home." He took off a heavy glove and extended his hand to Christopher.

Christopher focused his eyes and wondered how much wine he had tonight. "Home?" Christopher turned and pointed back toward The Oyster House and said, "But, I…" and stopped, realizing he was at the beginning of a new voyage. He was no longer cold; he took the scarf from around his neck and stuffed it into his coat pocket. He reached out his hand and allowed the Carriage Driver to help him step inside the carriage.

Fifty pounds lighter, he made himself comfortable in the back, unbuttoning his coat and the top button of his heavy shirt. “I came to life late,” he said. “It took me forever to figure it out.” He glanced at the back of the Carriage Driver, to see if he could tell if he was listening. He glanced around, “Maybe I did not figure it out. At first, I believed everything I heard. If someone told me something, I just took them at their word. Let me tell you as things unraveled, one time after another it began to dawn on me that what people said was not necessarily what they thought. So many things people said they did never were done, or how they felt was not near their true emotion.” Christopher took a breath, “I guess that is all lost now. Where are you taking me?”

The Carriage Driver felt like he was listening to an old friend. “If you think that, I suggest you don’t play poker with St. Peter.”

Christopher’s eyes shot up, and both men laughed. Christopher glanced back over his shoulder one last time. “Come on give. Where are you taking me?” Before he let the Carriage Driver speak he began again. “There is an old book by Robert Penn Warren, titled *A Place to Come To.* I always thought that would be a great name for a place people could arrive and just relax. Their time there would be pleasant with laughter, conversation, and maybe a Honkie Tonk piano player during evening hours, and, of course, good food.”

Nuelle turned onto the cobblestone path she had traveled so many times before. The Carriage Driver gave her rein. She knew the way as well as he did.

Christopher could not remember such peace as when traveling the cobblestone road. When the castle appeared on the horizon, he sat at the edge of his seat. “Is that where you are taking me?”

“If that is where you want to go, then that is where we will stop. It is all up to you."

It is all up to you. Chef Conant knew that. It was the hardest lesson he ever learned. He sat back and smiled.

Nuelle pulled to the front of the castle doors. A tall man wearing a black tuxedo opened the large double doors and walked toward the carriage as it stopped. The Carriage Driver climbed down and held out his hand to help his passenger down.

"Won't you join me?" asked Christopher. "Is this my castle?"

"Nuelle and I have a schedule to keep. Next time we are here, I will come in and see how you are doing in your new home. I hear that you know the secret to life." The Carriage Driver shook hands with Christopher and climbed back on board.

"The secret to life…I know the secret to life? Can you put that secret into words for me?" Christopher stood by the tall man waiting to bring him to his wing of the castle with its fully equipped kitchen.

The tall man had just finished carving in stone along the archway the words, "A Place to Come To."

Nuelle pulled close to the castle and turned the carriage back the way they came. When they again were next to Christopher, she stopped. The Carriage Driver tipped his hat back. "Put it into words you say. How is this? You get out of the pot what you put into it."

Christopher put his hands on his hips and laughed. "I knew that." He turned and followed the tall man through the castle doors.

The Carriage Driver[2] - Naming Names

The Carriage Driver heard a calling. He woke during the quiet hours after midnight. He climbed into his clothes and went down to check Nuelle.

Nuelle was awake and seemed to be in agreement that a walk down to their favorite spot looking out over the Atlantic was in order. There were campfires spotted along the stretch of beach. These were the campfires of the brave and the homeless. A canopy of stars embraced all who bothered to see.

"Nuelle?" A weak, astonished voice from the dark spoke. "Is that you?"

Startled, Nuelle raised high on her back legs at the sound of the voice. An ancient sound of a Confederate musket volley rang in her ears. The lead shot hit her rider in the left leg and right shoulder and he was thrown to the ground his Rough Rider slouch hat tumbled on the ground. Nuelle was not spared that day. The lead shot tore through her breast and found her heart.

He and his men found themselves on Bloody Lane on their last faithful day. It was just after dusk when the Rebels withdrew. In the dark, Captain Griffin Chaffey heard a voice in his ear. A young woman wearing flowing white whispered in his ear and he rose to his feet. His left pant leg blackened with his blood and the right side of his jacket was also soaked. He looked around and saw his beloved Nuelle lying on her side; he stood, grabbed the angel's hand and rushed to Nuelle.

"Come on, girl." He knelt beside Nuelle. "I need you. There is work to do." Bending closer, he whispered close to her ear. He collapsed to a sitting position. He looked around at the men he was leading. Boys in blue slumped still on the ground and over picket fences. Idle muzzles stared, as did idle eyes.

He stroked Nuelle's side. A translucent hand extended past the white sleeve she was wearing and touched Nuelle. She opened her eyes and staggered to her feet.

"Come with me. I'll show you the way." The angel extended her hand.

"Wait. What about these men?" He stood firm, resisting the lure of the angel.

"They are no longer your responsibility. They are out of your hands."

"I'm not leaving without them."

The angel disappeared, leaving the Captain and Nile standing overlooking the carnage of Bloody Lane. He went to his kit and took out an apple. He cut it into quarters, he fed two to Nuelle and ate the other two. He heard a noise. The boys were sitting up. Some were laughing. The Captain noticed they were clean, as were their uniforms.

The angel reappeared. "We have permission. They will sort it out at the nearest way-station."

The rest of the night was spent gathering each soldier and putting them on Nuelle's back. Nuelle and the Captain followed the angel. They were led to a cobblestone road that led to a way-station. The Captain and Nuelle worked through the night and the following day. Each trip brought one man home. Once they knew the way, the angel retired to other tasks.

The evening of the second day the last man in his Company was delivered to the way-station to await their judgment. The Captain felt tired. He wanted to go back home to his Boston. He and Nuelle walked side by side. On the road to Boston, he passed many men in need. In a field, he spotted an old carriage with the back wheel blown off from canon fire.

Looking at the carriage he had an idea. In the field, there was also canon lying torn from battle. He spent the day, with Nuelle's help retrieving wheels from the canon and fitting them to the carriage. He was now able to transport six to eight men at a time to the way station. Two years later the Captain and Nuelle found themselves back in Boston.

Neither Nuelle nor the Captain had thought of that night for over a hundred and fifty years.

The Carriage Driver patted Nuelle on the shoulder once her feet were back on the ground. He stepped forward to see who had spooked her.

Opaque in the black light stood a young Union soldier still wearing his Navy blue Kepi hat with cross rifles. "Captain? Nuelle? This can't be. I saw you fall outside Antietam. You couldn't have survived. None of us survived. Those rebels sure spit out the fire and brimstone on us." He paused. In the dark The Carriage Driver thought he saw tears in the young man's eyes.

"Can you help me? I am still trying to find my way home."

The Carriage Driver stood there momentarily speechless. He lifted his hat and ran his sleeve across his forehead. "I brought all my boys home to a way-station." Thoughts of the company roster ran through his mind. Doubt was at the forefront of his thoughts. We spent two days clearing Bloody Lane. Then two years were spent carrying all who were called."

"Captain, you brought me to the way-station. My case was dismissed and I left. Believe me walking down that cobblestone road alone was the hardest thing I ever did."

Nuelle swished her mane and wagged her tail.

The Carriage Driver said, "That was over a hundred and fifty years ago." He was having trouble grasping what was happening.

"Climb on."

"Captain, I can't ride a Captain's horse." The young man smiled.

The Carriage Driver took hold of the rein and lead Nuelle. The two men walked together and talked of the madness of war. Near dawn, they reached the stable. The Carriage Driver tossed the private a brush and picked up another for himself. They brushed down Nuelle and got her fed.

"I am going to have to give this some thought. Maybe after some sleep, I will figure an idea of how to help you."

The private agreed that some sleep was called for and sat leaning against the wall of the stall. The Carriage Driver went inside and got into his comfortable bed.

Hours later he went down to the stalls. "Look, we have a fare. Nuelle and I will be back as soon as we can. You rest here. I thought of something. Go upstairs and make yourself some breakfast." He harnessed Nuelle and they left. Running late for these appointments was never a good idea.

Returning from the Spring of Aganippe, The Carriage Driver disclosed his ideas to Nuelle. She nodded in agreement.

The private waited patiently for their return. He'd fixed himself a good meal, then cleaned up after himself. He cleaned out the stalls.

Reaching the stalls, The Carriage Driver climbed down and called out to the private. When he came to the side of the carriage, he held out his hand and assisted him into the back. He climbed on board and gave Nuelle her rein.

She knew the destination and took her time. She went through the Commons and could feel the energy being drawn to the private. The day was filled with promise. After a pleasant tour of the city, Nuelle made her way to Boylston Street and pulled up in front of the Massachusetts Historical Society and stopped.

The Carriage Diver climbed down and extended his hand to his fare. The private took it and climbed down.

"Follow me." The Captain said. "I think this is the place for you. You know so much and have so much to share. This is a place of history. This is your home to haunt."

The Carriage Driver[2] – Fly Me to the Moon

The one car garage, built in the 40's, held the fuselage of the airplane kit he had purchased. The wings leaned against the back wall near the workbench. Gene had pulled the fabric of the fuselage tight and with upholstery tacks secured it to the frame. On the bench, the blueprint sketches were held down with wrenches, cobwebs, and a coffee mug.

Years ago a neighbor had helped him hoist in the Volkswagen Beetle engine with the rust showing on the oil pan. The right wheel had gone flat. The project was in the eighth year. At eighty-eight Gene was moving slowly. He spent his time learning about the benefits of shark cartilage and chicken bone marrow supplements. On his good days, he worked on his airplane.

Looking down the hollow fuselage, you could see the aileron cables running down through metal eyes and turnbuckles as if they were Gene's personal spears of destiny. In the evenings, he would make his way to the garage, pull a ladder close to the cockpit and climb on board. His eyes no longer saw the incomplete control panel, with yet to be connected oil pressure and fuel gauges. He aimed to fly.

Inside the house, Gene studied the checklist. He made sure he knew how to connect the wings and made sure he had all the tools he needed with him to do that. Once the cockpit gauges were connected, and he broke down and bought a new tire and lined up Hank and his friend Mutt to bring him out to the road behind the fish hatchery; then he would have completed his checklist.

Two weeks later Gene was ready. At 6 AM Hank backed a rickety trailer up to the garage and with a winch towed the plane onto the trailer. Mutt with Hank's help secured the wings along the side. Gene walked slowly toward the trailer and set the toolbox on it. He walked back and carried a short ladder and laid it on the trailer. "Ready boys?" He called to the boys who exchanged glances.

They looked at this old man wearing greasy overalls and wiping his hands on a greasy rag. "Sure Gene. Hop in front." Mutt climbed on his motorbike and followed as Hank carefully pulled into the tree covered lane leading outside of town.

At 8:45 AM the wings were attached, and the boys paid the money promised them, plus the tools in the garage. Mutt stood by Hank's side and watched Gene set the small ladder next to the cockpit and ever so slowly climb inside. Mutt kept glancing at Hank. Hank watched Gene, fascinated. Finally, dirty Mutt had enough and climbed on his motorbike and left, being chased by a trail of dust.

Hank walked over to his old beat up pickup, leaned through the window and grabbed a smoke from his shirt pocket. He lit his cigarette and leaned against the side of his truck and waited. Hank liked Gene. He thought Gene had more gumption that almost any other man he had ever met. While helping with the plane he had learned about the many careers Gene had pursued.

The plane's engine started as Gene pulled the choke all the way out and turned the key. The prop sputtered to life and the plane shuttered. Gene tested the flaps, then waved his arm in goodbye. The plane wobbled down the flat dirt road and with some hesitation Gene was able to lift her into the sky.

He brought her to two hundred feet and made a slow circle looking out over the receding landscape. Then he climbed and headed out toward the Atlantic. He easily found the coastline and followed it south in the early morning sun.

In moments, he became lost in the rivalry between blues – both sea and sky swept over his senses. White laced waves lapped at him and currents of air pulled his plane higher through wisps of cloud. The chill in the air rushed past the windshield, hitting his face like the flush of his last kiss. The propeller twitched and stopped. It was the silence that broke the spell. He leaned forward and tapped his finger against the fuel gauge. Grateful eyes stared beyond his wrinkled face. Gene leveled the wings and began his long slow descent. He smiled, his last thoughts, of his late wife, Martha.

Griffin, the Carriage Driver, stood by the carriage and cut an apple into four pieces as he watched the tall, jaunty young man approach. His hands were in the pockets of his leather jacket and a scarf hung around his neck. He had a full head of golden hair and a princely smile. Griffin fed two pieces of apple to Nuelle and ate the other two.

Gene reached the carriage and took his hands out of his pockets and shook Griffin's hand. He walked over to Nuelle and patted her shoulder and said, "Hey, girl, I thought you might be a myth, but here you are to greet me."

Gene turned back to Griffin and took a close look at him. "So, you are The Carriage Driver. I read about you and always wondered if you could be true. News of your existence started out very slow. One person would hear about you, then tell another and another."

Griffin pushed his hat back on his head and beamed a smile. "So, now what do you think? Now that you are here, after all these years."

"If the stories are true, then you are willing to take me anywhere I want to go. Is that right?" Gene looked off into the infinite sky.

"If you can name it Nuelle and I will get you there." Griffin held out his hand to assist Gene into the carriage. "Do you know where you want to go?"

"First, I want to pick up Martha. She was taken much too young. I feel I left her all alone, and for that, I suffered for years. I would go out into my garage and work on my plane and thought about all the interesting times we had together. For a while, we owned a gold mine in Mexico and then after the war we ran a garage in Los Angeles. Those times of our youth were magical. What a great team, we made."

Griffin reached under the seat and brought out a book. He flipped through the pages, back and forth. "Oh, she was taken a long time ago. It says here that she wanted an assignment in the Great Hall with the artists and gypsies. The mosaic of the depiction of the Final Victory is breathtaking in scope if Martha was part of that, it was time well spent."

"I wonder if she will even remember me?" He opened and closed his hand, astonished that the flexibility had returned, and the joint deformity was gone. "I guess we can start there."

The sound of the carriage wheels against the cobblestone road was a symphony to Gene's ears, just like the roar of a double seat aircraft engine. He sat back, content with his life. He thought about the flat spots and the beautiful peaks. He thought about mornings in Mexico and bringing old engines back to life.

Gene leaned forward, "Captain, do you think after we picked up Martha, it would be possible for me to teach Angels to fly?"

The Carriage Driver[2] – Doc Angell

Doc Angell was nodding off in a chair, in the back office of the Memorial Veterinarian Hospital he founded five decades ago. At eighty-seven, he tired easily. He was serenaded by the rattle of a snoring chinchilla and the claws of cockatoos as they hopped on the floor of metal cages. Oscar, the office Ragamuffin cat, lay curled in his lap. He had worked late into the evening removing a metal wine bottle cap that had found its way into Ms. Murphy's pet pig.

His eyelids blinked once, then again slower. When his eyes reopened, the first thing he saw was vivid jade and emerald foliage. The sweet smell of rich soil engulfed him. Spring morning sunlight lent background to a pair of Blue-winged Macaws as they effortlessly glided around the garden. He walked with care through the hyacinth and daffodil and gazed with delight at a young pair of impala.

He pushed passed the rustling Canna leaf which then revealed the tail of a blue axanthic plains garter snake moving out of his way. A toco toucan pointed her long orange beak in his direction closely eyeing him while ignoring the male next to her on the branch. From Fuchsia draped branches, Coracias Caudatus puffed out her purple breast and sang to the morning.

A rain began, it was so light, Doc Angell watched as it modestly began to fall. The ground seemed to grab a hold of it and release it back into the air like puffs of mist for the plants. He looked around and spotted a tall tree. He went to it and with surprising agility climbed into the branches, disturbing a pair of nightingales. From the height of his new vantage point he could see the boundaries of the garden and a vast teeming, arid savannah beyond. He propped his legs up on a branch and leaned against the tree trunk. Intrigue crept into his consciousness; just beyond the boundaries there lurked savage strength and brutal hunger. He watched for hours.

Doc Angell climbed down and moved towards the boundaries. In an orchard he spotted a pair of humans frolicking. He paid them no mind and moved in earnest to get to the beyond. Some vines running along a portion of a wall provided his means of entering. As he dropped to the dry, rocky, earth he scooped a handful of dirt and let it run through his fingers. His taste of freedom, stronger than his need for safety.

Not yards from the boundary a pack of jackals had a cattle dog cornered. The dog holding them at bay with quick darts and determination, bled from his wounds. Angell glanced at the ground and picked up two jagged stones. He angled himself into position and let the first stone fly catching the flank of the jackal closest to him. The jackal leaped and turned; the second stone hit him on the snout and he fled; spooked the rest of the pack followed. The cattle dog eyed the strange beast that fought with him, but did not run. Doc Angell continued on and the dog trailed behind him. It began to rain, but there was no shelter.

Doc sensed the dog stop, and then in a flash it ran past him so low to the ground it did not seem possible. He continued on in the direction of the dog. In no time, a squirrel was brought to the strange beast and their bond was sealed. That night they shared raw squirrel and Doc cleaned the dog's wounds received in the fight with the jackals.

The A.M. Receptionist found Doc Angell's body. Ragamuffin cat long gone in search of heat, near an incubator. Doc Angell, now returned to his youth, rummaged through the clinic. He was filling a satchel. He had packed away a large box of wood matches and a straight razor, used occasionally in his work and an extra pair of socks. He filled a thick glass bottle with water and put that in the satchel. He went to the refrigerator and found a tomato and part of a cucumber that Sally brought for her salad. He stole them for the seeds.

Doc Angell checked in on Mrs. Murphy's pig. He scratched the cockatoo on the head and said 'goodbye.' He looked for the Ragamuffin cat, but could not find him to say goodbye. He turned slowly to survey his home of fifty years and thought about the good that was done here and thought of the sorrow.

He walked out the front door into the daylight. There was a stop to make. He did not want to go into the unknown without a sturdy knife to carry on his belt. He went to his home and into the garage, he found a long forgotten fishing tackle box and located an old knife; seeing the case holding hook and line he threw them into the satchel as well.

Nuelle and Griffin had made one trip to the castle this morning and were now waiting between the gas lamppost where many of their fare came to find them. Griffin stood by Nuelle and they just finished sharing an apple when The Carriage Driver spotted Doc Angell walking towards them. Griffin liked the cut of the man instantly and wondered where this young man was going to ask to be delivered.

Nuelle swished her tail and tossed her mane. Her instinct told her that this man had something special in mind. A sense of excitement swept through her. The Carriage Driver put his hand on her strong neck and gave a pat. He too felt the power this young man carried with him.

The Carriage Driver extended his hand and Doc Angell took it and stepped into the carriage. Griffin did not offer the blanket. He knew this man was not at all cold. After his fare settled back, he asked, "Have you decided where you want to go?"

"I do have some thoughts on the matter. I don't know what is possible." He hesitated. He leaned forward, "Can you take me to the beginning?"

Griffin held onto the reins. "To the beginning, do you mean where mankind began?"

"Yes," Doc Angell leaned back. "When the beast and the birds roamed the earth. To our paradise. Before we hid behind the word civilization."

Griffin climbed down and walked to Nuelle. Nuelle shock her head. He whispered into her ear, "It will be Ok, we went there once before." Then he climbed back into the carriage and Nuelle stepped away from the curb.

In no time at all The Carriage Driver, Nuell and Doc Angell were in a wilderness. Beasts roamed freely. Nuelle stopped near a watering hole where the grazing animals drank after the big cats drank at sunrise.

The Carriage Driver climbed down and helped Doc Angell with his satchel. The men shook hands and Griffin climbed in and left with a wave over his shoulder as they left.

Not twenty yards away a cattle dog was being attacked by a pack of jackals. Doc Angell picked up two jagged rocks and once closer flung with a good hefty pitch one of them at the jackal nearest. The jackal spun and seeing this unknown beast ran followed by the rest of the pack.

A woman stepped from her bath in the watering hole and stared at this new beast that had appeared. She pulled a wrap around herself and approached with some caution. She stared after the carriage and wondered who this god and his magnificent horse were that delivered, the man into her paradise.

The Carriage Driver[2] - Forever '51

"Keep an eye out for that yellow car," Mark said while pointing through the windshield. "She is drifting back and forth."

"I see her, and besides, if she hits us, we won't have to go to this party," Kathy shot back in a tone bordering on contempt.

"You have to admit; the party is a good idea. After all, she is our Mother, and she is turning eighty-eight."

Kathy glanced at her brother, who usually took a hard stance when it came to anything regarding their Mother. "You're just proud that my Goddaughter Kate thought of the idea of a party set in 1951."

"You have to admit, that you did not have a conversation with Toni for years that did not center on her life in the fifties. And don't call her Toni; she is your Mother for Christ sakes." Her right hand released the wheel and pivoted a punch on Mark's arm.

Mark rubbed his arm, in mock pain. "What's that make her; someplace in her early twenties? I barely remember my twenties."

"Yes, she would have been twenty-three; that is right after she had you by-the-way." Kathy tapped the brakes as the yellow car again drifted into her lane. "Kate's idea of inviting her friends from the Car Club was a good one. I am interested in seeing those restored old cars.

Kathy turned the corner, heading up the hill to Kate's place. She was happy to see the Car Club had arrived. It would be good to have a mix of younger people there at the house. Once parked, Kathy and Mark went inside, each carrying a large box with food.

Toni was sitting in a big overstuffed chair. Kathy was pleasantly surprised that the Car Club members all came 1950's era garb. The girls either wearing skirts to their calf or tight pants that ended at their calf. Boys in starched Levi's and square cut checkered shirts not tucked in.

A chill went up and down Mark's spine when he saw his Mother. Someone, he suspected Kate, dressed her in a full dress with full slip. She was wearing a wig, done up in a style resembling a wave. Toni was smiling ear to ear and talking to a young man who had braved sitting down in a chair next to her. He was holding a can of Pabst Blue Ribbon beer. His ironed and creased, blue jeans, clean white tee-shirt, and duck-tailed hairdo could not hide his lack of good sense from Mark.

In the backyard, Kate was coaching her husband Drew in the art of barbecuing hamburgers and orchestrating hot dogs off the grill. Many of the young members of the Car Club were hanging out in the backyard having a good time.

Julie, Mark and Kathy's sister arrived late. She walked inside and spotted the record player and carefully selected LP's grabbed up a Frank Sinatra album and set it to spinning. She then spotted Mark and zeroed in on him. "Mark," she called in a high pitched voice, "you should go dance with Mom." Julie ignored the painful blank look that flashed across his face. Grabbing his arm, "Come on. How many chances are you going to get?"

Mark found he was in a place that he was unable to cause a scene or tell his younger sister to buzz off. He walked over to where his Mother sat, and to the relief of the young man talking to her, asked her to dance.

The young man and his Mother stood. The young man headed toward the hamburgers and hot dogs and his friends. Mark and Toni moved in slow perky-circles on the hardwood floor of the living room to Frank Sinatra's, *You Make Me Feel So Young* playing on the phonograph. Julie, smiling like Batman's *Joker,* sat on the arm of a chair and took pictures with her phone.

"Bill, you should have picked a fast one. You know how much I like to be twirled." Toni said to her son, mistaking him for her first husband, Bill. She moved a little closer, "Maybe we can skip on out of here and go to the lake. Our days by the lake are so dear to me."

Kathy, who was watching, saw Mark stop. He looked pale. Kathy walked over and helped her Mother back to her chair. "Julie, come sit with her." She then took Mark's arm. "Let's get a burger. What happened?"

"She thought I was Bill. He left after only three years. I don't have any memories of him. You know that." He shook his head. A storm of family history thundered through his head.

Two couples came in and looked at the LPs. They picked a Miles Davis album and let it spin. The kids began to dance. Julie continued to snap pictures unaware that the mood in the room had shifted.

Kate with Drew close by for support walked over and sat on the arm of the chair where her grandmother sat. She watched her friends, dancing, with nice flowing movement to the vintage records. She held her grandmother's hand. She felt a light squeeze of her hand and then it went soft.

Kate stood and gently placed her grandmother's hand in her lap. She summoned Drew with her eyes, and the two of them went to find her father.

Griffin Chaffey, The Carriage Driver and Nuelle his white mare were waiting out front. He was out of the carriage looking at the yellow 1951 Chevy convertible and the 1951

Kaiser parked next to it. There were other classics parked on both sides of the street.

Moments later, Kathy, Julie and Mark were by their Mother's side. There was a quirky smile on her face.

The youngsters went out into the back yard and ate and drank their beer and someone moved the record player outside. They all felt more comfortable in the fifties than the Ought-teens.

The young lady in the full dress and slip, wearing her hair in a wave ran to Griffin's side. She saw Nuelle and the carriage, but wanted to sit behind the wheel of the yellow convertible first. The pain in all her joints was gone. Her skin was soft and smooth. The scar on her arm, she received in the car accident in 1970 was gone. She felt the sunshine. She climbed into the Chevrolet and put her hands on the wheel. She reached over and turned on the Philco. *Sixty Minute Man*, by the Dominoes, came on, and Toni's head moved in time, and she snapped her fingers. She reached over and turned the Philco all the way up.

She jumped from the car. Kicking her shoes off, she danced in the grass in her bare feet.

Mark, Kathy and Julie followed by the entire party walked out the front door and watched this twenty-something dancing, completely charged; without a care in the world.

Not to be outdone, the youngsters joined in. A title wave of exuberance flowed over Julie, Kathy and Mark and soon the girls were moving to the music.

Mark stood frozen. He watched Toni, age twenty-something, dancing. Her skirt twirled up, showing off her legs. A smile beamed from her face. Music blaring; emotions running high; for the first time in fifty years, Mark stood crying.

The Carriage Driver[2] – Man Unseen

Bruce Barton knew there were mean people in the world. He remembered when the boys in the neighborhood caught him on the way home from school. They jumped him and took off all his clothes down to his underpants and left him to walk the mile home. He still remembered Stephanie pointing and laughing at him. That happened in the fifth grade. The fifth grade is a tough grade to have to walk home in your underwear.

None of these children were nine anymore. Bruce still lived at home, but most everyone else had long ago grown up and moved away. They married, had children of their own and went to PTA meetings and complained about bullies in their neighborhood schools.

After the underwear incident, Bruce's mother had him moved into special classes with special needs children. The good news was that special needs children were driven back and forth to school on a 20 seat, yellow bus. The bad news is that never again did he hear another interesting talk about history or geography. He had always listened carefully about different places in the world. He liked the stories of the Indians and the Pilgrims. He liked the days the class did crafts with colored paper and glue.

Time passed. From age fourteen through sixteen, his school days were spent wrapping a plastic spoon and a plastic fork with a paper napkin and sealing them in a clear plastic bag. The members of his class were paid fourteen cents an hour for their trouble, by a thankful subcontractor to an airline supplier.

Bruce's mother passed when he was forty-two. Shortly after, men, sent by a bank came and cleaned out the possessions from the house and put Bruce out on the street. Within days, men emptied his pockets and his sixteen dollars stolen. He quickly learned how to scrounge for any food he could find. He learned to look for safe places to sleep. He learned to layer himself with newspaper to ward off the cold. It was not long before his permanent cough joined him. Bruce made it until age forty-five years on this earth.

Captain Griffin Chaffey, The Carriage Driver, stared at the page in the book that let him know his next assignment. He took special care polishing all the brass of the carriage. He groomed Nuelle, his white-haired mare and spoke in soft tones. He checked the blanket under the seat and put a basket with warm food and hot drink in the back seat.

He walked in front of the carriage leading Nuelle. He thought about inequalities and inhumanity. It was a cold night; his thoughts added to his darkness. He and Nuelle arrived in the smelly alley where the earthly body of Bruce sat slumped in death.

Griffin looked to the other end of the alley where a young man leaned, with his back and one foot, against the cold brick. He rubbed his face. The three-year-old beard was gone. He no longer wore ragged clothes and his shoes did not have holes in the souls. His hair was clean and neatly combed. His toothache was gone. He was doing math in his head. He figured that he made $80.00 for the five hundred and seventy hours of work packaging spoons and forks. He figured that the bank put him out of his Mother's house that only had seven more payments due until paid in full. He took a deep breath and realized his permanent cough was gone. He pushed off the wall and walked toward the Carriage Driver.

Griffin took an apple from his pocket and quartered it. When Bruce was at arm's length, he handed two pieces to him. Bruce looked at them and immediately fed them to Nuelle.

Griffin handed Bruce another quarter and the two men ate their piece in silence. When done, Griffin extended his hand,

and Bruce climbed into the carriage. He settled back into the plush seat. It was the most comfortable he had been since at his Mother's house.

"There is a blanket beneath the seat if you need it. There's warm food and a thermos of coffee in the basket by your side." Griffen gave Nuelle her rein. She slowly pulled the carriage out of the alley into the light.

Bruce ate a whole warm meatball sandwich and washed it down with hot coffee from a clean cup. Between bites, he said, "There ought to be rules for men to live by."

Griffin smiled.

"There are people who live on the streets and they may not get a full meal for weeks. And many of them, once they find some food, share it with their dogs. There was one man who lived beneath the Second Street bridge where I sometimes slept who would bath in the icy waters of the St. Charles so he could get clean enough to go to the blood bank and sell some blood. He would then buy food and feed all of us beneath the bridge." Bruce glanced up to see if The Carriage Driver was listening.

Griffin glanced over his shoulder. "There are some rules. Just too few seem to understand what they mean. That is why I carry so few passengers. Many people think they can atone for their lives at the end of it. Some even think donating some of their stolen money to their religious organizations makes their actions forgivable. Many of the religious organizations promote that idea. Believe me; there are no cash registers where we are going."

"I met so many of those. They steal from Monday through Saturday, and Sunday hand out a dime and go home feeling good about themselves." Bruce poured himself more coffee. "Do you have a cup with you? We can share this coffee."

"No, thanks," Griffin smiled. He did not expect generosity from this man.

Nuelle swished her tail and tossed her white mane. She thought she knew what her fare was going to ask. She turned up the cobblestone road leading to the castle. The wheels clicked and rattled, making their music.

Arriving at the castle, Griffin climbed down and held out his hand for Bruce. Bruce was a little surprised at the tall man in the tuxedo that walked through the wide wooden doors toward them. He looked over his shoulder at Griffin. "Can you wait for just a little while?"

"Yes, I can wait. I have no other passengers scheduled today."

The tall man led Bruce inside and invited him to sit at a table near the fireplace. "The cook will make you anything you would like. Please be seated."

"Can you lead me to the kitchen?" Bruce asked.

"Why yes, this way." The two men walked into the kitchen where the kitchen staff stopped what they were doing.

It was the cook that spoke, "Sir, can we help you?"

"Yes, if it is possible can I have a basket of sandwiches?"

A quizzical look came over the cook's face. One of the kitchen helpers leaned close to his ear and whispered something. He looked at her and beamed a smile. Several of the staff began gathering food and formed a line to make sandwiches.

In a very short time, Bruce carried out a basket of sandwiches and handed them to Griffin. "Can you deliver these to the people beneath the Second Street bridge on the way back?"

Griffin took the basket and set it in the back of the carriage. The two men exchanged a brotherly hug. Griffin climbed into the carriage, and Bruce walked back inside.

Griffin heard Bruce ask the man in the tuxedo if it would be possible for him to have a teaching position somewhere.

The Carriage Driver[2] – The Ghastly Knight

The carriage sat idle between the gas lamps in a hazy mist of a cold Boston gloom. Nuelle heard the hoof falls a moment before Griffin, who was dozing. Nuelle startled, pulled sharply to her right, nearly upsetting the carriage. In doing so, she freed herself from the carriage and faced the direction of what was approaching.

Griffin, now fully awake, climbed down, trying to assess what was going on. The hoofbeats grew louder as they approached. There appeared through the fog a pale horse and pale rider. The willowy rider wore a scraggly white beard and from this viewpoint a pot used for cooking upon his head. The base of the lance he carried rested on a plate suspended from his saddle.

The riders aged horse stood two hands taller than Nuelle. Had Griffin not held the reins that Nuelle still had from her collar, he was sure that Nuelle would make quick work of horse and rider.

"You are no longer needed!" The old man rocked feebly on his horse. After he had spoken, it seemed like he chased a flea that called his beard home.

"What are you saying? Just who sent you here?" Griffin tensed listening for other riders. Strange things happen in the in-between.

"Look at your book. When was the last time you had a fare? People don't need you. This new crowd, they are all about today. What happened yesterday does not interest them, and besides, they don't believe what is told to them. Their generation thinks there will be no tomorrow." The rider sat tall carrying his accusation, still scratching at his beard. His horse stepped to his right, trying to get a better angle on Nuelle. The lance was moved slightly forward, to be more menacing.

Griffin scratched his cheek, more from the power of suggestion, than anything else. When he realized he was doing so, his hand dropped to his side. "Plenty of people still need us," he touched Nuelle on her shoulder. She did not take her eyes off the rider.

"They will always need us. We are their deliverance: to their hope, their faith, their salvation."

"Yes, you were. But, we are near the end of the last generation that finds a need for those attributes. Today and over the many lands I roam, the people want brand names, digital pleasures, they want access to glitter. They want energy efficiency, and corporate hierarchy, and microbrewery. Abandon your carriage old man," the old rider adjusted the pan he was wearing on his head. "You are outdated. What they are told to do, to earn a ride from you is hard work – no one wants hard work. You sit in that carriage in the cold, in the fog or the snow waiting; and for what? One rider a week? You work all hours; are there more people coming out of the churches on Sunday or the night clubs and bars on Friday and Saturday nights? Your pride and honor have evaporated into nothing."

Griffin tired of the conversation. He walked over to the carriage and returned it parallel to the curb. He checked the rigging and guided Nuelle back into position. Both Nuelle and Griffin kept an eye on the man with the lance.

"What are you doing? You heard me. You are no longer needed! There are no good people left. Those that threw off the offerings of processions, and refused their positions in the corporate worlds or military adventurism are the closest we have."

Griffin climbed to the seat and grabbed his book. He walked over to Nuelle and took an apple out of his pocket and cut it into four pieces. He fed two pieces to Nuelle and walked over to the aged white beast and her rider and fed two pieces to her.

He opened the book and held it up. The Ghastly Knight tipped the handle of the pan out of his way and lifted the book close to his face. After reading the entry, he handed the book back to the Carriage Driver and readjusted his pot. Out of the misty morning fog, a short brown burro walked and took a position alongside the ancient white nag.

The burro surprised the old man. Nuelle, her head turned to watch was also surprised. She was first to hear the quiet footsteps as they approached. She picked up the sound of small slippers walking on the Boston sidewalk.

The boy could not have been older than six. He wore those cheery scrubs that children in hospitals are given to wear. These were light blue and covered with pictures of windmills. He approached the carriage. Looking at the Carriage Driver, he said, "Mister. Can you help me?"

Griffin climbed down and extended his hand. "Once you climb onto the carriage I can deliver you anywhere you want to go. But you can wait. There is no hurry."

"Yes, sir. My mom can no longer stand my pain. So, I need to go." It had not escaped the boy's attention that there stood an old knight, just like in his book.

"Have you said your goodbyes? Did you remember your father and brothers and sisters?"

"Yes, sir. I remembered."

Griffin extended his hand and helped the boy into the carriage.

All his pain left his body. He leaned over the side, staring at the old knight with his scraggly white beard and jousting lance. He stood and grabbed the rail that was behind the carriage driver's seat rest. "Am I here."

Griffin smiled. "Yes, son, you are here."

The boy hopped down and with amazing agility climbed onto the brown burro. The two riders turned away from the Carriage Driver and Nuelle, and walked into the fog.

"You can walk faster than that Rocinante," was the last thing Griffin heard the old knight say.

In the cold, foggy air, the boy saw looming up, a spire that belonged to the Old South Church.

"Stop. "You are no longer needed!" The old knight brought his lance down to attack. He kicked at the sides of his old horse, who obliged his Master's bidding by walking slowly forward, followed closely by the burro. "Stop, I say. Didn't you hear me." The ferocious giant glared down at him in practiced silence.

The boy looked back over his shoulder, hoping to see the Carriage Driver. The fog had closed in around them. "Sir, I chose you! I want you to teach me. We can stop for the day. Let me make you some tea. Teach me of honor, teach me the ways of courtesy. Tell me about the days of old, when honesty existed. I want to hear about when strength went into brave acts rather than bullying."

The old man looked at the boy. With the greatest of care, he climbed down from his horse. Once his feet were on the ground, he rubbed his back.

"Gather some wood for a fire, would you," he told the boy.

He took off his hat and poured water in it to heat. He dug around for some tea and found some. Once the water was prepared to heat, both the boy and the old man sat on the cold ground. Their steeds were secured to a municipal trash collecting container.

The old man began, "When I was young, the earth was clean. For as far as the eye could see both the earth and the sun provided all that was required in the kingdom of man...," the old man stopped and looked at the boy, he cleared his throat. "Let's save that for another time. Did you ever hear the story about, *The Knight of the White Moon*?"

The fog slowly burned away.

The Carriage Driver[2] - The Gutter Boy

It had been three days since Dylan took half of his mother's beating. When the drunken brawl finally collapsed into silence, he quietly went out into the streets and walked away from the emotional chaos. The first two nights he slept in Franklin Park, but the rumblings of a broken civilization and dark, shivery shadows scared him more than the replacement his mother had found for his father.

He wandered away from his anger and fears, shrouded in the illusion of safety, down Harvard Street towards Dorchester. At dusk, he spotted a Patrol Car on Geneva Avenue and ducked into an alley. He rummaged through a rubbish bin, behind a deli and found some food. Once he had eaten, he curled into a ball and fell asleep behind the dumpster.

In the wee hours after midnight Dylan was startled awake, as he was dragged by his ankles out from behind the dumpster. Three of the midnight crawlers spotted him and began to kick and slug him, just for the fun. Dylan kept his kidneys protected, and endured the abuse. The beating stopped as quickly as it began.

Griffin Chaffey cast a big shadow down the alley as he approached. The three young thugs thought better than test this man approaching them.

Griffin picked the boy up and walked out of the alley. He did not climb into the carriage. Nuelle walked behind him matching his pace.

"Put me down," Dylan protested.

Griffin did as requested. "Let's talk while we walk. Is that OK with you?"

"Yeah, I guess so." He felt along his rib cage, where a solid kick had landed. He squirmed a bit at his touch.

"The world can be a very dark place. If you are not careful, you can be swept away in the darkness. No one would even know. Part of your task as a man is not to become one of the nameless, faceless people. That is not as easy as it sounds. A cornerstone of a good life is to find people to take care of, and in return, they take care of you."

Dylan listened. None of his experience in life so far reflected what this stranger was telling him.

As if reading Dylan's mind, Griffin said, "There are constructive ways to raise a family. In fact, you owe it to yourself in the future to remember how you were treated and make sure that you give better than you received. Don't get me wrong; everyone has flaws. One thing we all need to work on is not to let our flaws, guide us. We also have incredible strength inside of us. More than you can understand at this point in your life.

"Where are we going?" Dylan asked.

"We are going to cross over an invisible line. And you are never going to have to fall back beyond that line. If you cross it, it will be your choice. That might not make any sense, but you will see what I mean." When Giffin turned a corner, Nuelle, pulling the carriage followed at a distance.

The two walked and talked. Griffin grew to like Dylan on their walk. They turned a corner and found themselves on a street lined with Brownstone homes on each side.

"Follow me," Griffin instructed.

The two walked up the stairs and knocked at the door. It was still the early hours of the morning, but Griffin was confident that someone would answer the door.

A moment later a man in his forties opened the front door. Seeing Dylan, he opened the door wide and said, "Come in."

He glanced at Griffin and the three entered his home. "I'm Doctor Geller." He reached his right hand out to Griffin.

The doctor looked at the cut above Dylan's eye. He felt along his rib cage. "Come this way." He led them to an office with a couch. "Take a seat there," he pointed to the couch. "Take your shirt off."

A pretty woman in a housecoat to her ankles walked into the room. "What is it, Daniel?" She looked at Dylan and felt immersed in a pool of well-being upon seeing Griffin.

"I am going to put on some coffee," Daniel told his wife. "Will you stitch the cut above his eye? Then I am going to reset that broken rib and wrap him. He is not going to like it."

Mrs. Daniel Geller was also a doctor. The two married at the beginning of their Intern years. She opened a drawer and took out what she needed. She handed Dylan a gauze pad and said, "Hold this over your eye. I am going to spray something on the wound; you will feel a tickle as I close the wound. OK?"

Dylan, not seeing any way around it said, "OK," and covered his eye.

Ann began, she expected a little jump from Dylan, but he did not budge, or make a sound. His suppressed emotions made her curious.

Daniel walked into the room carrying a tray which held a pot of coffee and cups. He watched Ann quickly and efficiently stitch the cut above the eyebrow. Daniel set the tray down, "My turn," he told Dylan. "This is going to hurt, and there is no spray for it, but once done, that sharp stabbing feeling you have been feeling will stop. Ready?"

The doctor did his work. Ann again noticed the boy did not scream or jump. Daniel finished and wrapped Dylan's ribs.

Daniel conferred with Ann. "Excuse us." The two walked out of earshot of Dylan and Griffin. When they returned a few moments later, they returned. It was Ann that asked the question, "We know a man who runs a school for boys. He is a friend of ours. Dylan, would you be interested in meeting him? Daniel and I are the doctors for the school, so we know many of the boys. We hope you say yes. He is on his way over to talk to you."

Dylan looked at the three adults. The pain over his eye stopped, and the throbbing in his chest was much better. He looked from the doctors to Griffin where his eyes rested. "There is no way that thank you is enough."

Ann looked at Griffin, "I want to hug you. Would that be OK?"

Daniel smiled to the room in general as Ann walked over and wrapped her arms around Griffin. "I get such a feeling from being near you."

Griffin turned to Dylan. "I did not hear your answer. Are you staying? And will you attend the school these two recommended?"

"Yes, sir. I will give it a try."

Griffin walked to Doctor Geller and shook his hand. "I'll find my way out."

Ann watched, she was sure she saw an aura of light that surrounded this man. "Will we see you again?"

Griffin turned at the door, "Not for a long, long time." He opened the door and walked out.

Ann walked to the door behind him and watched as Nuelle pulled the carriage to the curb in front of their home. Griffin stopped near Nuelle and took an apple from his coat pocket. He cut it into four pieces and fed two to Nuelle and ate the other two. She watched Griffin climb in and take the reins.

He adjusted himself in the seat, then turned around and looked at his fare. "Ok?" He asked.

Dylan's Mother smiled and said, "thank you."

The Carriage Driver[2] - The Man With The Flowers

Finn Grady carried a bouquet of forget-me-not. White petals fell like teardrops, adorning the path behind him as he walked across Lawrence Street into Phipps Street Burying Ground. His habit over the years was to don his Sunday best and visit his wife, Nicole Grace.

The soles of his shoes were thin, the seat of his trousers threadbare. The suit coat had threads sticking out at the collar from feeble repair. His thinning hair was covered by his fedora, left over from his working days. The years had turned his pencil mustache white.

Her black granite stone was simple. It had her name engraved, and the dates and Finn had paid extra for a sculpted rose. He reached the site and with slow deliberation sat down. He took one stem from the bouquet and set it on top of the stone.

He pulled a small plastic bottle of water from his jacket pocket and a sandwich wrapped in wax paper. He sprinkled some water on the grass in front of the stone. He pulled Saturday's newspaper from his pocket and set it down. Then he reached into the pocket designed to hold a wallet and pulled out a piece of paper. In a soft voice he read:

Time is different now

The oranges soften in the bowl

Flowers send for ladybugs

To use them for a stroll

Life lingers in the balance

Night hours take their toll

Sundays find me sitting here

Upon this grassy knoll

Entangled in our silence

Time, no measure of a soul

Friends still sing your praises

and your efforts to console

Grief fueled my journey; gone

our days of ole, I pray they're

only moments left, before

we'll once again be whole

He folded the piece of paper and reached for his pocket. He thought he would put it in her hat box later with the others. He leaned against Nicole Grace and passed.

A cemetery is an unlikely place to die. So much so, that Finn Grady caused a stir with the locals. Jacob Hurd (1758) was the first to arrive; alongside him, stood his son John (1809). "Welcome," Jacob bellowed. "We could use some new members around here. Me and my son are goldsmiths and silversmiths. Not much gold shows up here to work on and just a spot of silver. We made the most beautiful pieces."

John Hurd, noticed Benjamin Gorman (1855) walking toward them. "Hang on to your wallet. He was a Congressman. He never saw a dollar that he did not think he could spend better than the bloke who earned it."

Finn Grady took in the sight of these three men. Each wearing breeches and white leggings, vests and long coats and shoes with large buckles. Jacob wore a white wig.

Congressman Gorman started to speak, but just then, buxom Molly Hunnewell approached. Jacob, John, and Benjamin stopped looking at Finn and watched her. Her red dress with empire waist caught and held their attention.

Molly, flaunting her assets came up close to Finn and ran the fingers of her right hand along Finn's cheek. "When you get tired of listening to these bores, come on by. I'm right over there," she pointed in the direction she came. "I am warm and soft, and busy on cold Boston nights." She flashed a smile and went and leaned against a stone marked John Harvard. Her presence disturbed the occupant.

Harvard (1638) arrived angrily, "What's the meaning of this intrusion?! Jacob, John? Gorman, I have told you before to stay in your section."

Gorman ignored him.

"Molly, I have asked you not to put your, ah-er, posterior on my stone. Blasted, what are you all doing here?" He tugged at the ends of his vest and eyed Finn. He stepped a bit closer to Finn and said, "What are you doing here? Souls go elsewhere."

A heavyset man, one of the Frothingham appeared from the far corner of Phipps Street Burying Ground. His clothes were unkempt and his hair stringy. "What's all the excitement? What is everyone doing out?"

Finn took a step back, the others arrived neatly attired, and for the most part were well mannered. But this man, heavy and slouched at the shoulders, ill clothed and bad teeth disturbed him.

Frothingham said, “Come with me. It is a lot more friendly over on our side. Not so snobbish and formal. A better class of people over there, if I do say so myself. We are earthy.”

Jeffery Grady, Finn Grady’s son, lived off Bunker Hill St. across from Doherty Park. This Sunday morning he was napping in front of the television. At 10:30 A.M. he sat straight up, rubbed his eyes and wondered what was wrong in the world. He reached for the phone and called his father’s number.

Nuelle and the Carriage Driver were up early today. Griffin took his time and groomed Nuelle and polished the carriage. It was going to be a long day. Once ready, he began to climb onto the carriage. He stopped, pet Nuelle on her flank and walked back into his house. He had forgotten Nuelle’s apple.

The carriage moved slowly and deliberately. They made their way to the castle and picked up their passenger. By request, Nicole Grace made arrangements to meet her husband. The streets of Boston had a freshness to them that Nicole had forgotten.

Nuelle made her way to Phipps Street and the entrance to the burying ground. The carriage wheels announced their arrival.

Finn’s guest all began moving toward the carriage; they were full of envy and regret. Frothingham approached Nuelle, who swished her mane and shook her head.

Griffin stopped the carriage and climbed down. Finn seeing Nicole, walked through the spirits. Griffin held out his hand, and Finn climbed into the carriage. He greeted Nicole Grace with a warm, gently kiss.

"There is a blanket beneath the seat if you need it."

Jacob and John drew near to Griffin, with painful, longing looks on their faces. Gorman and Molly walked back toward Molly's arm in arm. With the excitement subsiding, the rest wandered to their stones.

Jeffery Grady unable to reach his father, by phone, decided to go and see if he could find him. He knew that his father visited his mother on Sundays. Nuelle with a nice easy gate left the entrance of Phipps Street Burying Ground.

The body of Finn Grady leaned up against the stone of Nicole Grace Grady a smile on his face. Jeffery found him. Finn was holding a piece of paper in his hand.

In the carriage, Nicole leaned against Finn, "I know just where we can go first. Are you ready for our next adventure? The first thing you are going to find out is, time is different now."

He handed her the remaining bouquet of forget-me-not.

After the grief of the arrangements and the sadness of the funeral, the task of cleaning out his father's apartment fell to Jeffery. The task took longer than expected when he found a hat box belonging to his mother. It was filled with love poems written over the years to Nicole Grace.

Tears streamed down his face for hours, as the life of this frail man that was his father unfolded before him. At the time, Jeffery did not know that it would take two years to get a thick book of poetry published. The title, *Time is Different Now.*

The Carriage Driver[2] - The Book Thief

Preface

It seems the characters that appeared in, *'The Man with the Flowers,'* felt there was more to be said. If anyone finds themselves here at 'The Book Thief,' who has not read the first portion, you may be lost. I don't think I have coupled carriage driver stories before. Though in January, Sister Sarah, made two appearances *Sister Sarah's Secret* and *Sister Sarah's Miracles.* I have taken license with this episode, and it may feel out of place.

And now:

The Book Thief

In the hours after midnight, Ezekiel Frothingham leaned against his stone at Phipps Street Burying Ground and slowly turned the pages of the book he'd stolen from under the seat of the carriage that had come to pick up Finn Grady. Molly Hunnewell crouched near him. They both overlooked their disgust for each other as they tried to share the same space in front of the book, and searched in vain for an entry with their names. There was a damp chill in the air, and the gas lantern casts a dim glow on the thick, rich pages.

The locals at the cemetery awakened by the presence of Finn Grady's soul and the arrival of the seraph driving a carriage pulled by a flawless white mare had been unable to return to their rest. Their old feelings of abandonment and shame returned. Jacob Hurd (1758), a goldsmith in life and his son John (1809) a silversmith, paced near Frothingham's stone waiting. They did not dare come closer, fearing a thrashing from Frothingham or a straddling by Molly. Their chance to inspect the book would have to wait.

"What have you done now, Ezekiel? You holding a book is a laughable sight. Maybe if you read faster, the rest of us could get a look before he returns." It was John Harvard (1638) who spoke.

Frothingham glanced up through long, dirty, stringy hair and looked straight at Harvard, "You're mighty proud of those words of yours. See'n you'n me lives here in the same neighborhood I don't see what's so high and mighty about your words. What makes you think he is going to return? Everyone was looking at the soul of that man and the innocent woman. If he would'a saw me, there'd been hell to pay."

One time congressman, Benjamin Gorman (1855), roused from his undertaking of going through the pockets of the newcomer smirked from the shadows where he stood and waited for Harvard's reply.

"Rest assured, Ezekiel Frothingham; he will be back. And you can see," he raised his arms, encompassing this piece of the scorekeeper's garden, "that our bill has been presented. You are just mad because you were denied entrance to the celestial hierarchy and received no explanation. Like the rest of us, you were scooped up without glorious ceremony and dumped here. Now, the rest of us would also like to double check for our names, so get on with it."

Molly touched Frothingham's hand and made him turn the page. She was aware that all eyes were on the book tonight. As were her own.

Captain Griffin Chaffey woke early. Something nagged at him. He climbed out of bed and dressed quickly. He tugged on his boots and went to the stall where Nuelle slept. He searched the carriage, and as he sensed, the book was missing. They shared an apple and then he led Nuelle outside and climbed on her back. They rushed toward Phipps Street Burying Ground.

God took the form of an owl to go unnoticed during the goings on. As a precaution, the graveyard cat was turned to stone during the proceedings. Owl thought, *When will they learn, you are not judged by what was put in your way, but what was put in your heart.*

When they arrived, Griffin dismounted, and they entered side by side. In the unnatural darkness, Nuelle's coat emitted a glow that enhanced Griffin's aura. Griffin spotted a subdued flush of light from the gas lamp on the far side and led Nuelle towards it.

Molly and Frothingham stood when Nuelle arrived with Griffin by her side. The Hurds moved closer to the book; Gorman stepped from the shadows and John Harvard stayed put a few feet away from the others. Though these were the spirits present when the carriage driver arrived the first time, there were others listening from the shadows. An old sea captain who drowned while whaling stood heavy on an oak peg leg. Other various brigand and prowlers crowded the shadows, away from the flickering light.

"We knew you would return," John Harvard spoke. "You cannot blame us." He pointed, "I have been over there since 1638. The world goes by, quietly at first, then louder and louder as machines thunder away at their industry. You sir, cannot have time to contemplate the questions of the universe as you go about your business. How do we know the mistakes that you have made won't destroy all that we had here in this vast abundance?"

Molly took a step forward, "I did not get to finish looking through the book. Why isn't my name there? All I did is make my way with what I was given. My appearance was pleasing to men. I turned that fact into money to feed myself. Is it my fault that my name is not entered into the book? Just what chance did Molly Hunnewell have in a world dominated by men?"

Griffin let the reins go. He walked over to Frothingham and extended his hand for the book. He stared into the man's empty eyes. He saw no hope reflected. He looked at the last entry in his book. There was an appointment to be made that morning.

There was nothing in Frothingham makeup, or past that gave him any idea as to what to do. He looked around for some ideas from those around him. Seeing none, he handed the book to Griffin.

It was Gorman, who spoke next, "What makes that book yours? It collectively belongs to the people and should be shared equally. We all walk along the paths that are put before us. We all spend six days a week with the turmoil and struggle of life and one day of preaching. The system has as much to do with our pitiful existence as the words spoken from a book. Aren't all men created equal?"

The weakness of his words reached Griffin's ears. Blame fell here and there, but not squarely anywhere. Griffin glimpsed a shooting star and sensed the first breath of dawn. He turned and took the reins to walk Nuelle back to the carriage.

"Just where are you going? We have asked you many questions, and you have not answered a single one of them. Who is responsible for putting our names in this book?" John Harvard demanded to know.

"You are," was Captain Griffin Chaffey's reply.

He walked out of the burial ground and headed toward Mass General. It was a long walk, but he did not want to be late for his appointment. When he arrived near the entrance, an eight-year-old girl wearing her nightgown and clutching a teddy bear stood there waiting. Her guardian angel, kneeling by her was just finishing the braid in her hair and adjusting her garland. The girl's smile beamed her gifts of love. There was no question in Griffin's mind as why her name was in the book. He reached her and said, "Do you mind going for a ride on Nuelle's back?"

"Oh, please, that would be so nice?" Her face broadcast joy. Her pure heart groomed for the next part of her journey was full of spirit.

Griffin pulled an apple from his jacket pocket and cut it into pieces. He handed the girl two pieces and fed two to Nuelle. The three made their way to the castle in the sky.

The Carriage Driver[2] - The Weathervane

It was with grief that Bess moved her Mother into the rest home. She postponed the decision for a year or maybe longer than practical. The small kitchen fire sealed the deal. Bess moved fast and decisively. She researched every rest home within driving distance of their home, and she and her husband selected what they thought the best one. No surprise, the home where therapy dogs were there to greet them, won their hearts.

Bess visited regularly and knew the staff and many of the seniors by name. She was cheerful to all. The family celebrated their holidays there, and she attended all the special events scheduled for the home to engage the guests.

This evening in the final moments of their visit, Bess reached over and took her Mother's hand and flashed her "I love you," smile. The two glowed with a lifetime of memories. "Momma, remember our little cove near Key West? You know, that day? I wore a pair of shorts and a tee-shirt with stripes and a pair of leather soled sandals. The ones where a little strap near the toes was the only thing that kept them on. You were about thirty and a youthful beauty, in a flowery summer dress. Daddy told me, that dress always made his heart beat fast.

It was a gorgeous day on the Atlantic shoreline. There was a picnic basket filled with treats just waiting until we got hungry. Dad steadied the skiff as we all climbed aboard; oh, what a nice time we had with some light fishing and gay laughter filled the clean, clear air. Gulls circled, waiting the chance at a fish head or the last piece of a hot dog bun.

I carried my brand new transistor radio; I never parted with it. The radio played *Tie Me Kangaroo Down Sport*, and *Puff the Magic Wagon*. And Jimmy Gilmer sang about a *Sugar Shack*. The waves rocked the boat, making you, me, and Dad feel the comfort and grandness that life had to offer. The sun splashed its power and made the red snapper bite.

You opened the basket and handed Dad a cold beer. And pulled from the ice, a little wax bottle and handed it to me; it held a sugary flavored drink. I just needed to bite the wax shaped bottle cap lid off. It offered one gulp of refreshment. Then I chewed the wax, getting the last remnant of sugar. With pleasure, I then spit it into the ocean, put my hand in the water and rubbed the saltwater over my small face. There were no more content people to be found anywhere in the world. Those were days like no other. Remember Momma?"

Lisa often closed her eyes and went back there, leaving her wheelchair-bound body far behind. She treasured the time spent with her family and the time spent in the seclusion of the banyan trees with her husband, Matt. She watched children ride their bikes into the wind, freedom blowing through their hair. Baseball cards clipped with clothes pins, so they flapped in the spokes of the wheels sent sputtering sound through the branches of trees.

She watched a stream of children running after the ice cream truck, waving their dimes in the air to get him to stop. And she saw the clothes waving on the lines. The Flame Trees, in full bloom, added a dash of color against the blue of the sky and the sea.

Bess watched the gentlest of smiles come across Lisa's face and felt the lightness of being spread through her.

Angels visit us. After a time, Captain Griffin Chaffey noted many of the places in his area where he stopped frequently. The home where Lisa spent her last moment was such a place. He had visited this home often. Many of the guests, over the last hundred years, had seen his carriage. They found a weather-vane that depicted his stops and had it installed on the roof to guide him. The guests thought that would prevent the *least little chance he might forget the way.*

Griffin was in no hurry. When he reached the curb outside the home, he climbed down, he and Nuelle shared an apple. He reached underneath the front seat and found the brush he had placed there. He knew the elderly needed more time to prepare. He brushed Nuelle and spoke softly to her. Both liked that extra time and extra attention they shared with each other.

A short time after they arrived, the front door opened. Lisa was thirty again, in a summer dress. Bess walked Lisa to the carriage; Griffin put his hand out for her. Lisa turned and paused, she took a step closer to Bess and embraced her. "This is as far as you go, for now."

There was no question in Bess' mind where her Mother would choose to go.

First, she would find Matt; then they would find a boat to sail back in time to the Key West of her youth.

Matt was not in the first place Lisa looked. Nuelle and Griffin loved their little vacation and took in the sights like tourists.

Islamorada Island is where they found him. He had built a small house on the beach, with covered porches on two sides. Then he planted two palm trees the exact distance apart to suspend a hammock for two. There was a supply of coconuts stacked, and a sea breeze to greet Lisa. Calypso music danced along the inviting waves from the distant village.

Nuelle stopped, and Griffin climbed down. He held out his hand, and Lisa stepped down with all the grace of royalty. Matt rushed to the carriage. He was young and strong and tan. That Navy smile, that she fell in love with, filled his face, and he grabbed her and gave her a kiss that made up for many years of absence.

For Griffin's sake, Lisa pretended some embarrassment. Her eyes are wide and her smile broad.

Nuelle waved her rich white mane and her tail. Griffin stepped up into the carriage and took one last look around. Then gave Nuelle her rein. When Griffin glanced back over his shoulder, he saw, Lisa's summer dress laying on the sand and both Lisa and Matt running into the warm blue surf, enjoying the nature before them.

Epilogue:

I borrowed heavily from the history of 'one of our own,' to compile this story. The picture of the weather-vane was the inspiration. I was shocked to see it and amazed at the location upon the roof of a rest home. As usual, I don't feel that I gave the story justice.

In every sense of the words, this story represents our history; all locations of the country enjoyed the innocence of postwar freedom. Our flag waved above all the government offices with pride. The United States was respected throughout the free world and viewed with envy by many in countries that were not free. We were a beacon of light and welcomed with open arms all those from foreign lands that made their way here seeking protection inside our borders.

We felt safe. We knew our neighbors. We talked over back fences. Faith in our future was not questioned. We sold food to the rest of the world. We were an industrial giant. We placed trust in our leaders. We worked hard.

Postscript: Griffin found time to ride Nuelle in the surf before returning to Boston. It did them both a world of good.

The Carriage Driver[2] - The Twelfth Man

Carl Blankman felt a shadow over him all morning. He woke early. This was going to be his big day. Nothing was going to stop him. He had worked hard to get here. *This is the biggest game I am ever going to officiate,* he told himself. It was like a dream, he had lined coached, and was a referee for many seasons. The New England Patriarchs (*sic*) made it to the championship again, and he was going to be on the field.

He threw his uniform and his shoes with rubber cleats in a small travel bag. He tried to ignore the peculiar feeling that seemed to be following him around this morning. He reminded himself to eat less pizza and have fewer beers with the boys the night before a big game.

He took the bus into Foxborough. It dropped him off at the entrance to Gillette Stadium. The early morning atmosphere in this large arena made Carl feel small and somehow vulnerable. The stadium filled him with awe. He glanced over his shoulder a few times as he walked down the dark tunnel leading to the locker rooms where he would change.

He liked this stadium. The fans were always fired up and ready to go. They cheered for their team. He would go out onto the field and greet a few of the groundsmen and then go say 'hi' to a few of the food vendors. He liked being there to say hello to the team's cheerleaders as they arrived. He referred to game day *as his day at the cathedral.*

The fans began to arrive. A slow trickle at first, then a river of fans marched in with their banners and their spirit. Some painted their faces red, white, and blue; some painted their stomachs. Young girls wore shirts with flags to display their support.

Soon the announcements began. The air filled with anticipation, the crowd hummed with excitement. *Carl Blankman was on the field,* he thought. It did not matter to him that the championship team was also on the field. The quarterback Tom *something or other* was the city's hero.

Carl, hands braced on his knees as the first ball was hiked, inspected the line. The ball snapped, and a lateral pass to a tight end and the ball was coming in his direction.

He moved fast to follow, keeping a sharp eye on the defensive lineman that was two steps away from the first tackle of the game. And 'Pow,' the crack of the hit could be heard in the first rows.

Carl gave a quick glance around him; he was still unable to shake the feeling someone was following him all morning. The teams lined up; the ball hiked; Tom took quick steps to his right and threw a thirty-yard pass to his wide open receiver.

Carl yanked the yellow flag from his pocket and tossed it into the air. He stood straight and put both hands on his head, signaling 'illegal participation,' or an extra man on the field.

The ball floated effortlessly into the waiting hands of the receiver who stepped into the end zone for a touchdown. When the crowd finished cheering Carl Blankman lay dead. The back judge and field judge conferred. They agreed neither of them saw the extra man on the field. They signaled the side judge who lifted his hands in the air to signal the touchdown.

Tom was kneeling by Carl, and most of the offense huddled around him.

The opponent's disheartened defensive team went to the sidelines. Their offense milled about the sideline waiting to take the field.

The Boston sky was plain gray, colored by a child with a single crayon. The air hung still, and people took short breaths as if sharing the air. They went about in shocked silence. Blue eyed girls wept, and brown eyed men took no notice. The light in the City of Champions now, lost in reflection.

Captain Griffin Chaffey, the Carriage Driver, had never been called to Foxborough before. He found the place easily and drove the carriage through the parking lot and through the tunnel that leads to the field. He drove onto the field and right next to the where Carl Blankman waited. It would be a moment before Carl would realize his ride had arrived.

Carl stared at his body lying on the ground and heard the ambulance pull right up on the thirty-yard line. Two EMTs rolled a gurney next to Carl and placed his body on it. Then they moved him off the field. Carl stared at the faces on the field. The twelfth man was there. The shadow that had followed him all morning stood there smiling.

Griffin climbed down and extended his hand to Carl. A few people in the stadium stood and watched Nuelle swish her tail and toss her magnificent white mane. Order began to be restored. "Are you comfortable?" Griffin asked.

"As long as we are here, could you drive between the goal posts?" He stood and pointed to the uprights.

"Sure thing, Carl."

When Nuelle reached the uprights, those few in the crowd that could see her, stood up and let out the loudest cheer their lungs could offer.

Once under the goal post, Carl stood in the back of the carriage and threw both hands up in the air. The biggest victory sign he could muster.

The announcer asked for a round of applause from the crowd. And the game of life resumed. The shadow went into the stadium; he spotted A.E. Sage from Framingham, whose time quickly approached.

A roar rose up from the stadium. Tom, *something or other,* just ran the ball into the end zone from the nine-yard line. The fans went wild. The quarterback was going to walk away with another AFC championship. The standby referee shot both hands up in the air to signal the touchdown. The points went up on the board. The Seattle Sea Doves were going to go home defeated, their feathers ruffled.

Carl turned back, from looking over his shoulder. He leaned close to Griffin. "What harm would it be to go and watch the rest of the game?" His eyes open wide, with the prospect.

He pulled lightly on the left rein. Nuelle listening to the whole conversation began turning back in the direction of the stadium. The three of them could watch from a vantage point directly behind the goal post.

Number 3 came walking onto the field. At two hundred and fifteen pounds Stephen, the New England Patriarchs' field goal kicker was set to add more points to the scoreboard. The ball was hiked, set and with a precise blow sailed through the uprights. Carl caught the ball as it sailed into his arms.

Carl, now holding the ball, with a smile on his face and amazement in his eyes, said, "I am concerned about the timing of this event. This puts a damper on my big day. My very biggest day. And now, in the record book, there is going to be an asterisk that says, 'Carl Blankman died during the game.' And then the record book is going to say, 'his very last call was a mistake. There was no twelfth man on the field.' If people remember me at all, that is how they will remember me."

Griffin responded, "You get it right, in the record book that matters."

Nuelle worried, a little, about the after-game traffic on Patriot Place.

The Carriage Driver[2] - Inherit the Earth

Linda carried her loneliness like a stone. The vow of love, long forgotten and their home was now just a house in rubble and tears. She wore courage like a badge. Her family supported her, but could not reach deep enough to sustain her.

The last day her husband was in the house was a rough one. He came home and consumed the beer in the refrigerator. The more he drank, the madder he became. His inadequacy as a husband and his failure as a man was all blamed on his wife.

When she arrived home, she immediately became his target. The beer can, half filled with warm beer went sailing at her as she entered. The spray hit her, and she heard him laughing.

"That's it, get out," she screamed. "Get out; I am calling the police. Get out."

He rushed across the room, he grabbed her shirt and tore it open. He slapped her. His aim - make her small, humiliate her and make himself feel better about the nothingness of his existence. Anger dimmed his mind.

That had happened months ago. Linda filled her time, throwing herself into helping preserve a place where peacocks roamed. It was a local park, and the birds brought much joy to all those that stopped by to slow down the breakneck pace of their lives.

The paperwork needed to escape her harsh reality was being hammered out. She had been successful avoiding her husband other than the arbitration meetings; she was obligated to attend them. She glanced at her watch, and left Peacock Park, for just such a meeting.

Griffin Chaffey stood in the stall next to Nuelle and brushed her. He took so much pride in her and treated her like royalty. The carriage that had sustained his spirit for so long was cleaned and polished to a point suitable for a queen. When it was time, he climbed into the seat and made his way over to the parking lot of a local divorce lawyer.

The meeting inside was heated. The husband had a couple of belts of alcohol, just to bolster his mood. He was not going to give an inch in his demands. 'Who does she think she is? I am the man,' he told himself over and over. Not even his lawyer liked being in his presence.

The two lawyers called the meeting to a close. They got nowhere today. They called for a cooling off period, and set another appointment for the following week.

As both Linda and her soon to be ex-husband went to the parking lot the argument began again. "You are not getting what you want. You are never getting what you want. Do you hear me?"

"What I want is to be rid of you. And that will happen sooner than you think. I've already met someone that treats me better than you ever treated me."

Nuelle and the Carriage Driver turned into the parking lot. They witnessed the unfolding of the next forty-five seconds in shocked silence.

The husband pulled a revolver from beneath his shirt and fired, hitting his target.

Nuelle pulled forward quickly. She inadvertently ran the wheel of the carriage over the husband's foot, crushing it.

Griffin climbed down and went to Linda, who was sitting on the asphalt of the parking lot. She looked at her body lying there on the ground, and then to the husband limping away. She heard him cursing. The whole scene was surreal. Her eyes rested upon Nuelle and the burden on her heart was lifted.

She checked herself and found no bullet holes. Her clothes were not stained with blood. A man with the gentleness of a lifelong loved one knelt beside her. She was trying to absorb the moments of her transition.

"Can you stand yet?" Griffin asked. He stood up and offered his hand.

Linda stood. She looked in all directions. She could see her old car. She watched as her ex's car rushed out of the lot, in a big hurry.

Nuelle waited patiently. Her ear twitched, and her white mane waved.

Linda was bathed in the peace.

"I know this is sudden. You are in an entirely safe place now. All your pain will be forgotten. There will never again, be an instance of humiliation." Griffin extended his hand.

"I will be back," Linda called and ran off to the park that she loved and where she was going to meet a man with a gentle soul named Jason. They had intended to share lunch. When she reached the park, she spotted Jason sitting on a bench. Her smile filled her face, as he was feeding one of the peacocks she had named Wilbur.

She sat down next to him. It did not go unnoticed that the beautiful white horse pulling the carriage arrived and pulled beneath a shade tree to wait. "Dear man," she began, "I thank you for your kindness. Your shoulder was just what I needed. Your heart is going to be bruised in the next few hours. For that I am sorry. We did not have time to get to know each other's hearts, but what I did learn impressed me very much." She took his face in her hands and presented a gentle kiss.

Jason smiled at the thought of her. He grabbed his cell phone and dialed her number, but there was no answer.

Griffin stepped down from the carriage when she stood. When she arrived under the shade tree, he put out his hand to assist her into the carriage.

Linda stepped up and took a seat.

"Do you know where you want to go?" Griffin asked.

She noticed her clothing had changed. She was in a gown of the softest material she ever felt. Her hair, which she usually wore down was freshly combed, tucked in the back, and adorned with a garland fit for a queen.

"Could I go somewhere that there are shade trees? And perhaps a small body of water? A place where people can go to relax if only for part of their day. Where gentleness and the wild creatures of nature can be in harmony together. I don't mean lions and tigers. But perhaps some grazing animals and peacocks with their attractive feathers and rituals."

"I know just the place," Griffin told her as he stepped down from the carriage. He extended his hand, and she stepped down into her kingdom. He offered the crook of his arm, which she took. They walked through the park, under an archway of tree branches. Two proud male peacocks spread their feathers to acknowledge her presence. The tails of two squirrels formed question marks at her early arrival. A trio of butterflies waved their wings in greeting. A throne awaited her in the midst of the trees.

In the branch of a nearby tree, a wise old owl surveyed the scene and once satisfied flew off in the direction of the castle.

Griffin climbed back aboard and gave Nuelle her rein. When she made a turn, that would lead her away from their home; he was curious, but let her go. There was a second turn, then a third. Then up ahead, he spotted three small black metal buggies, pulled by a small black horse. Little men wearing black sat waiting for a fare.

Nuelle cantered by and with deliberate intent bumped one carriage driven by the competition and trotted away. The men that were all dressed the same, with handsome black boots and tails draped over their shoulders. They did not take the insult lightly and rushed after Nuelle and Griffin.

Griffin was enjoying this and knew Nuelle was up to something. She easily outpaced the smaller horses and the trio of black cabs and their drivers. Up one street and across another she went. She followed her instinct and arrived in front of a bar where the ex-husband was hiding out, having his last drink.

She pulled to a stop and waited for the trio of black cabs to arrive. They stopped and climbed down, angry. Nuelle dashed away, as she judged her mission accomplished. Griffin laughed as he watched the three competing drivers decide to enter the bar rather than continue the pursuit.

The three took stools next to the ex-husband. They introduced themselves and waited for him to finish his drink.

The Carriage Driver[2] - State

The bleak light of a bare electric bulb casts long shadows into the grim space where Joshua wrote out his final thoughts.

'Dear Lord,

It's me, Joshua; we haven't spoken in twenty-eight years since they put me in here. You must have had a reason, 'cause you know I was with Betty Sue, down by the river when that crime they convicted me of was going on. You made women, and you made summer nights, so how could that be my crime. I put a lot of thought into that and have not come up with an answer.

I promised myself I wouldn't talk to you again until I was getting out. Well, the same Doctor who kept telling me that nothing was the matter, and I lost all my privileges 'cause I couldn't work; is now telling me I am going to die soon. I went from 'nothing is wrong', to death's door with no medical attention in here.

After twenty-eight years, that door slamming shut at night still shakes me to my core. Everything has been taken from me. The only thing I have that I can take with me is the memory of the slamming of that metal door.

This is my first and last prayer in twenty-eight years; I am asking if hell has metal doors?

Joshua'

Joshua Harding's written prayer was placed in his file. The front of his folder was stamped, 'Deceased,' and filed. The State was done with him. He died in the cell they gave him when he was thirty-two years old. There were no pictures taped to his walls and only one book on his shelf.

Buried in the local newspaper was a report of his passing, with a recap of the brutal 1988 crime. The remaining family members of the victim celebrated the news; even the cousin who committed the crime.

Griffin walked toward the castle, to which so many trips had been made over the years. The trips were often filled with both sadness and joy. Today after dropping off his fare, a horseman took Nuelle and told Griffin he would brush her and feed her. She could rest before returning. Upon entering the castle doors, he was greeted and brought to a room where a counselor waited.

"Griffin, we have a most unusual case. It is not often we seek consent for an assignment. But we thought we would give you a chance to decline. If you have checked your book, you will see there is no name there. We are giving you an opportunity to turn us down, though we know you will not."

The counselor looked more confused than concerned. "What is it, sir? What could be so shameful?"

"A soul is waiting for you at Suffolk County House of Corrections. You have never been there before. We checked." He pushed a map across the table. "You have been near it several times." The counselor leaned forward, "Do you have a problem picking up a soul from a prison?"

"It sounds like he may have broken some of man's rules, but this meeting tells me you don't think he has broken any rules here. If that is the case, I don't have any problem at all. How long has the soul been waiting?" Griffin waited for a response.

"His spirit was ready a long time ago; now his body has released his innocent soul. He is waiting now. You'll recognize him."

Joshua paced, seven, eight, he stopped, nine. He turned back again – eight, nine. For close to three decades when he paced, he took eight steps and turned back in his confinement. And now he could take nine steps.

Griffin knew the location: he had passed the prison many times. Nuelle was brushed; her harness was cleaned and polished. All Griffin's passengers were treated with great care. He felt honored with the privilege bestowed upon him. Turning down Brandon Street still took some effort. The mere weight of the walls oppressed the spirit and wickedness seeped from the concrete.

Joshua watched Nuelle and the Carriage Driver approach on the otherwise deserted street. He watched as the carriage pulled close to the curb and Griffin climbed down. Griffin took an apple from his pocket and shared it with Nuelle.

"Are you here for me?" Joshua asked.

Griffin gave Nuelle a pat on her cheek. "We are here to transport you on the next portion of your journey."

"Are you taking me to hell in a carriage? Is there even injustice in death?" Joshua felt for the first time that he could speak his mind. He realized that the pain in his joints was gone, and he was a young man again. He put his hand to his face and found the long scar he received behind the wall was gone.

Griffin offered his hand to Joshua. "Once you step inside, we will take you anywhere you want to go. Have you given this any thought?"

"All I thought about for years is that man created all the evil in the world. It is masked behind the rhetoric of darkness, but it is a thin veil. The big struggle is within us. We learned how to hunt by watching animals, and now we prey on each other. We failed to learn the lesson that the animals hunted for food: man hunts for pleasure."

Griffin listened; Nuelle twitched her ears and waved her white tail. Just as Griffin was going to lower his hand, Joshua took it and stepped into the carriage.

"Can you take me away from this wall?"

Nuelle was given her rein and pulled from the curb. She listened to every word both men spoke.

"The man that shared the space with me died, and I spent the last nine years in the space alone. We did not talk much. He lived in his head. I guess, I lived in mine. How can two people share such a small space and not talk to each other? He had one book that his son sent to him. It was called, *Big Sky Country,* something like that. For a short time, he talked about going there when he was released. It was a picture book, but had some words too.

There were mountain ranges, so pristine that it looked like you could reach out your hand and pick them up. The sky raced a thousand miles in all directions. It looked like a place where a man could be free. Lakes with garlands of pine trees were tucked away in the valleys. It looked like a mighty fine place."

Nuelle made her way along the cobblestone path that leads to the castle. Her steps were slow and deliberate. The wheels rang out their peaceful cadence. It was a chilly day in Boston, but the passenger did not seem to notice.

Joshua Harding's, sat up straight once the castle was in view, "You are tricking me, aren't you? Those walls look as thick as the ones that I just left." He looked around thinking to leap from the carriage.

Griffin signaled Nuelle to stop. "That is a way station. We think we know where you want to go. We can go in this carriage if you wish. But we have a guide that can take you there in the fashion of the old west. You'll go on horseback through some beautiful country. Is that OK with you?"

Joshua sat back. "There was a place called Paradise Valley. It was close to the Yellowstone River. The book talked about some hot springs nearby. The man who shared the space said it all sounded perfect; it only needed a cheerleader boot-camp by the lake every summer."

Jim Bailey, who waited at the castle for his love to arrive, volunteered to guide Joshua Harding to Paradise Valley. He waited with horses and gear to escort this man who so much had been denied him in life.

The two men were introduced. "I thought we would ride above the Great Lakes, then drop down into North Dakota and see some of Minnesota. "What do you think? There's lots of wide open country to see. And we are in no hurry."

Joshua mounted a horse both sturdy and gentle, and his new journey began.

The Carriage Driver[2] - The Whale's Tale

Duarte's mother asked him not to go out on the sea. But a teenage boy is full of himself. Besides the sea this morning was as smooth as his girlfriend's skin and the wind as warm as her breath against his neck. He climbed aboard the little sailing dinghy and headed toward the horizon.

The craft glided smoothly under his sure hand and in no time at all, the land had receded. The universe of misty air and foamy sea engulfed him. He opened Nordhoff's, Pitcairn's Island and began to read.

When he woke, the shutters had closed on the sky, and the sun put away. He sat up straight and looked at the choppy sea. It only took Duarte a minute to regain his senses. He took his bearings; he steadied the tiller and pointed the bow west toward home. He soon found a spiteful wind would not let him race his race. The sea had changed and swells lifted and lowered the bow. He trimmed the sail to keep from being turned on his side.

He grabbed the rope that tied to a plastic bucket on one end and nailed to the wooden seat on the other and began to bail water. A sudden bump yanked him from the urgency of bailing.

The bow dipped, and he took on more water. He leaped from the craft to save it. Clinging to the side; he was able to reach the small pail and bailed. Across the short width of his floating world rose the head of a whale. Duarte stared into the depths of the eye facing him. The movement lifted and emptied the boat. Duarte climbed in.

On his knees, looking over the side, he saw that the whale carried a nested blanket of plastic netting. He grabbed a skinning knife from the sheath nailed by the leather belt loop to the seat and reached over the side and pulled his small skiff closer. He attacked the netting, and it began to pull free. With one last slash, the tangled mesh sank away.

For his efforts, he took on water. He centered himself and again bailed. When the water was about ankle deep, he laid back to catch his breath. As he did a wave tumbled him and carried him down into a soft world. The whale watched from a short distance and sang out a song that said, 'follow me.' She sunk her head and dived.

The whale came alongside the floating body. Near him, the pages of Pitcairn's Island turned at the touch of the current. The words lifted from the paper and drifted about the boy. She nudged the body; he did not hear when she again sang out; 'follow me.'

Griffin Chaffey readied their carriage. Nuelle was cleaned and brushed. Her white mane glistened. For the first time that he could remember, the book sent him to one of his and Nuelle's favorite places. The entry reads, 'The Five Sisters,' a little strip of land near the Boston shore, where it was common for Nuelle and Griffin to walk in the hours of early morning.

When they arrived, Griffin climbed down, and he and Nuelle shared an apple. The wind was brisk. Griffin watched little halos, spidering along the horizon. He did not know what was causing them until a Coast Guard helicopter that was out on a search and rescue mission returning for fuel flew overhead.

Two women came along holding a lantern and climbed cautiously out along the breakwater. Griffin watched as they huddled under a blanket together. First one held their beckon high, then the other. When they tired, they set their lamp before them and waited.

Hades claimed Duarte for his own, since no land gods were near. The whale after conferring with Poseidon negotiated with Hades. After the location of a sunken whaling ship, with fifteen trapped souls was revealed, she was allowed to guide Duarte's spirit to the shore.

The women had not waited long when the massive tail of a whale emerged from the surface. The whale called out a greeting to them and sunk quietly back into the blue-green depths of her freedom.

Duarte climbed the rocks of the breakwater and stopped, surprised to see his Mother and his girl waiting. He sat down with them and talked to each one. First, he told his mother that he loved her and that he was sorry that she would now carry his grief. He touched his lips to her cheek.

He moved closer to his girl. He kissed her and embraced her. Down on one knee, he whispered into her ear and then hugged his last goodbye.

It was when he stood that he saw the magnificent beast that was Nuelle. Duarte leaped and jumped along the breakwater stones with the confidence of a young man. He made his way toward the carriage. He arrived, dripping wet. The white pants, he wore clung to him; on his face a boyish grin.

"I sure screwed that up," Duarte spoke with youthful enthusiasm.

"Forces beyond comprehension have brought you to this spot. But I have to tell you that if you made mistakes, the cards still fell in your favor. Wait here."

Griffin walked toward the jetty. With guided feet, he walked out to where the two women huddled. When he arrived, the two women realized they were ready for shelter. Neither saw Griffin as he guided them back to safer ground. He watched them walk away and wondered if he would see them again.

Duarte leaned against a wheel of the carriage and wept as the women walked away. His girl carried the now extinguished lantern. Griffin came by his side and extended his hand to step up into the carriage.

"Where are you taking me?" Duarte wiped at his tears.

"Nuelle and I will take you wherever you want to go," his hand still offered. "You are very young, so you likely did not give this any thought. Your decision is not permanent; if you select a path and tire of it, you can select another." Griffin put his hand down when Duarte took a step away.

"You mean there are no restrictions?"

"I suppose you can call them restrictions. They are the same restrictions that you have always followed. I won't deliver you to Belle Watling's brothel in Atlanta. But perhaps a sailing ship would be to your liking. Have you given this any thought at all?"

Duarte paced before the carriage, "A sailing ship. Perhaps, the Esmeralda, no. I could sail with Darwin on the HMS Beagle or maybe the Pequod, no, hmm. Both the HMS Bounty, the HMS Endeavour, were fine ships."

Griffin took his turn leaning on the wheel. "There is always the Jolly Roger," Griffin added to the list. Griffin thought Duarte looked like he was thinking hard. "There is the Pilgrim." He offered.

"I've got it, USS Constitution. I want to spend every hour that the USS Constitution spent at sea on her decks. Is that possible?" Duarte walked over and faced Griffin.

"I suppose anything is possible. You know she is docked right here in The Boston Navy Yard? They nicknamed her, *Old-Ironsides.* She has a rich history. Are you sure you can handle her?"

"Handle Her? I don't want to be the Captain. I want to climb into the rigging, and to when necessary, man the cannons. I want to fight the Barbary Coast pirates and hear the cannons roar at Tripoli."

Griffin put out his hand, and Duarte climbed aboard.

Nuelle took a look toward dawn and the now calm sea. She slowly turned the carriage toward Old Charleston and made her way to the berth where Duarte would spend years on the first leg of his new journey.

The Carriage Driver[2] – And Match

Bud Worth owned Bud Worth Express, LLC. Four shiny vans that crisscrossed Boston. The business was light pickup and delivery. He insisted his drivers wear slacks and white shirts and that they were courtesy both to his clients and on the road. He paid more than the local Teamsters and replaced two vans every two years. He wanted his fleet bright and clean. He had competitors, and as much as possible stayed on friendly terms with them. He often boasted, "I know every backdoor to every small business in the city." And it was true. In quieter times he told those that would listen, "I have money, but it was earned one nickel at a time."

His passion was not commerce or intrastate business law, which he knew inside out. He set aside Sundays for time on the courts of the Boston Athletic Club over on Boylston St. As the American poet, Edwin Arlington Robinson noted, in *Richard Cory*, Bud Worth was imperially thin. His height and build served him well on the tennis courts. Inside him lay the urge to win and here under the sun was his battleground.

In the clubhouse, if he was spoken of at all, they said he was a percentage player. He often won because of his snappy one-handed backhand and by holding the serve as long as possible. Many talented players lost to Bud Worth, as he crowded the net and wore them down.

In the locker room this morning, two other members mentioned to Bud, that Lilith was here looking for a game. Not many would play her. Bud had played Lilith before and won. They battled hard, and both he and Lilith limped away from them, to fight another day. "If you see her, tell her, I am game," he called out.

He tied his shoe laces tight. Then slipped on his wristbands and headband. He gave his Wilson racquet a spin, then another. He almost felt it become just an extension of his arm.

He walked out to the courts, spotted Lilith and went and sat opposite of her. They acknowledged each other with a small lift of their racquets. The couple on the court were running into his reservation time; he sat and waited, without comment, as they played out their final point.

Bud drove out of his mind the thoughts that crept in; *he had beaten her before*, *her gender was no match for his,* and finally *this is my day*. He stood and limbered up as the couple gathered their gear and with light apologies cleared the court.

Bud felt the pulsating heat coming from the asphalt. Lilith spun her racquet and won; she chose to serve. Knowing Bud liked the serve, she hoped for an early psychological advantage. With an easy lob into the air, she smashed a brutaliser, aimed right at Bud's chest.

Bud's move puts him on the ground; he spun to see the ball land outside, 'fault,' he called.

Lilith smiled, her legs now glowed like polished furniture. She bounced the ball a couple of times, then served. Bud sent the ball sailing back to her; with a backhand as smooth as the devil's tongue the ball came back. On the ninth return, the players on the adjacent court stopped their game and watched.

Bud's tennis shoe scraped the asphalt, and he was a second late to set before getting the ball lobbed back to Lilith. She planted her feet, thighs taut, and with a two handed backhand, the ball blasted between his feet. "Fifteen-love," Lilith called. She picked up a towel and patted her neck.

Bud stared at her: she seemed bigger than he remembered and stronger. He grabbed a towel and wiped the sweat from his face. The court seemed different to him today. As each ball returned to him, he glimpsed little transgressions in his life. He envisioned small shards of flames on the court. When the second volley ended, Lilith called, "Thirty-love."

The game that was going on in the court on the other side came to a halt, and the couple stood by and watched the fire pit of a match going on.

Lilith grabbed a bottle of water and poured it over her head. Her grin and leopard eyes sent chills to the couples watching.

She served the ball to the right side, to see it returned. She knew he had slowed down; she easily placed the ball to the far left of the court. She had him running, right, then left, right-left. She controlled the court without the need for a couple of steps in either direction. People were watching out the clubhouse windows.

Lilith won the first game. Bud came back strong and managed to squeak out a win in the second. Many now were gathered in the courts on either side.

The third game pounded along. Every point cost a pound of flesh. The court felt so hot to Bud. His perspiration was not keeping him cool. Bud fought and scraped knees and elbows, letting nothing get by him. He needed one point to her two to win the set.

A high lob brought her racquet down like a hammer, and the ball fired passed the quick-footed Bud Worth. He reached for a collar that was not there. He stumbled and fell as the ball bounced passed him. "Deuce," Lilith called. And picked up another ball and was set to serve.

She looked up and saw Bud Worth collapse. She ran and leaped over the net and rushed to him. "Get up; I'll win you fair and square."

Nuelle pulled the carriage to the curb in front of the Boston Athletic Club. Griffin climbed down and stopped to share an apple with her. He'd not been inside the club, but when he walked through he followed the crowd to Bud.

Lilith was hovering over him when Griffin arrived. When Griffin came to them on the court, she looked up and said, "I won him. Our magic is greater than yours. Humanity has chosen."

Griffin smiled and helped Bud Worth to his feet. He looked at Lilith and said, "It was a fault, you lose."

"You weren't here; you don't know." Her face turned her natural red.

"These people all witnessed it. The whole clubhouse watched." And to Bud, "Are you ready to go?" The two of them walked toward the clubhouse doors.

Lilith gathered her things and walked toward the showers. It was early; she thought perhaps she still had time to entice one of the bored young wives. Her work was never done.

Griffin reached the carriage. Nuelle waved her white tail and shook her mane.

Bud admired the carriage. He appreciated the high level of maintenance. The upholstery was clean and crisp. He admired the polished brass, and lacquered woodwork. He walked to Nuelle and said a hello. "We are in the same business; light pick up and delivery." Walking back to Griffin he asked, "Is there a special fee for Sunday pickup?" He smiled at his wit.

Griffin held out his hand, and Bud stepped into the carriage. He noticed that he no longer wore the tennis outfit. He wore gabardine slacks and a white linen shirt. He sported a Panama hat and Italian loafers. He lifted a pair of sunglasses from the shirt pocket and put them on. It looked like he was going through the front door at last.

The Carriage Driver[2] - 8mm life

The winds of time kicked up the last of the dust at the end of Fuoad's road. The anesthesia brought him to a theater that long ago he visited once. When he arrived at the theater, a beautiful young usher escorted him to his seat. Fouad thought he recognized her, but he was old, and his mind played tricks.His first girl smiled, kissed him on the cheek and left him alone in the dark.

The curtains pulled to either side, and an eight-millimeter movie began to play. The thought that his life was going to play out for him in 8mm amused him. Fuoad looked right and left. He was alone.

The screen showed a desert village where he lived as a boy. He was assigned tending to the animals and as he grew every farmer in walking distance brought their sick animals to him. The screen showed him taking care of both cattle and camels. A noise caught his attention. A small dog ran down the aisle and jumped in Fouad's lap. A beautiful young woman entered and took a seat in the back.

The clicking sound again was interrupted when the happiest golden retriever found him and took the seat next to him. Another lady with a regal air found a seat in the back. She kept a close eye on her golden retriever.

The reel ended, and a note appeared on the screen, 'One moment, Please,' Fuoad reached over and scratched the Golden Retriever behind the ear.

Again the movie began. Two parrots flew into the row and sat on the back of the seats behind the first animals. A gentleman with a patch over one eye asked permission to sit with the ladies. The screen showed Fuoad having, a fight with his father, then a rust covered freighter leaving port of his home country. An overbearing father stood on the pier watching the ship leave.

When the next 'One Moment, Please,' sign appeared, two young women Fuoad dated in his college days herded in a flock of rabbits. The dogs paid them no mind. The back rows were filling up; as were the seats throughout the theater. Small animals of every description roamed around. Their owners chatted and kept an eye on their pets.

The screen depicted a small wedding. The bride was young and contented. Fuoad leaned forward at the memory. He needed an embrace, and the golden retriever was happy to be there for his friend.

At the fifth reel, the theater was pandemonium. Birds flew, dogs dashed after rabbits, both rabbit and dog were enjoying themselves.

Fuoad thought he saw his wife of long ago, leaving the theater as the reel came to an end.

The owners in ones and twos came to give their last respects to the man who, after doing all he could to save them, had seen them through the final moments of their pets' lives. Many in attendance returned to their journey with their pets by their sides. In the end, Fuoad sat in the dark alone.

He was no longer in the theater. He was aware of people around him. Aware of their haste, and the clinking of instruments. A monitor that had been beeping somewhere in the depths of his consciousness ceased. He became aware of the silence.

Captain Griffin Chaffey tapped his finger on the name in the book. A name that was out of the ordinary appeared, Fuoad R. Abdell. He closed the book and checked over Nuelle again and inspected the carriage. He reminded himself that he drove the carriage. He walked Nuelle, pulling the carriage out of the stable and checked his pocket to make sure he carried an apple.

They arrived in front of Mass General. They posted themselves between the two gas lamp post, and Griffin climbed down and shared an apple with Nuelle. "We are going to have an enjoyable ride; I can feel it."

Coming down the stairs in front of the hospital, a handsome man dressed like a desert prince right out of a movie came toward Griffin and Nuelle. Griffin stood by the step to the carriage and waited.

"Are you here for me?" This man with deep set sparkling eyes asked.

"Yes, we are to take you to wherever you want to go."

The man paused, then took Griffin's outstretched hand and climbed in. Griffin did not offer the blanket at his feet. The man looked perfectly comfortable and perfectly content. He had the look of a man who had found his mission in life early and then spent his life pursuing his purpose. It is a very rare look to find on a man's face.

"Do you know where you wish to be taken?"

Fuoad leaned forward. "When I was a boy, at night the men would gather sitting on a rug and talked with my grandfather. I would sit quietly and listen. They spoke of a land in the Nile Valley where date trees and palms pulled the heat from the air and turned it into treats.

It was a land where the water was drawn from so deep in the earth that it came to the well head cold to the lips and as sweet as the nectar made by the work of the bees. The water was so valued that every drop was savored.

They spoke of a land unchanged since the Pharos and the forty days road where the caravans inched their way between the ocean of sand and life-giving waters.

They boasted that there were no women more beautiful than those that bathed in sunset amongst the reeds in the oasis. And they quarreled whether the sun draping the skies with orange and amber made their skin more brilliant. The perfume from the purple flowers along the banks drifted to those in the water.

In the evenings the Falcons were turned loose to retrieve meat for the traveler's fires. Tents of all sizes and colors protected the nomads. Skins of the big wild cats made many a resting place for the weary. The sky was a dome of stars, and you could reach out and embrace the moon.

The name of this place is Kharga Oasis. A deep depression, in the vast sand ocean. A valley with all the wealth a man needs for a simple life. The old men spoke, as if, all the wealth a man needs can be carried in their hearts. His shoulders are used to carry food to his animals, and his labor is traded raising animals to feed his family. They would lift their voices in praise, and thanks for clean air and deep waters."

Fuoad looked up at the Carriage Driver, "You are not what I expected. I had in mind, perhaps a flying carpet." He smiled at his little joke.

Griffin tipped his hat back. "Many stories handed down to mankind tell about what comes next in their journey. If you need a flying carpet to make this part of your reward more fulfilling, then one can be provided."

It was Griffin's turn to smile at his little joke. "Many of the stories, maybe all of them, came out of the desert over the centuries. But tell me this, can there be different Gods for different people? There can be different journeys. We have many more roads to travel. And we have traveled centuries and millenniums, and we have trails full of discarded gods."

Nuelle pulled from the curb, and the wheels rang out along the cobblestones. She was heading toward the castle. She would let someone else figure out how to cross an ocean of sand.

The Carriage Driver[2] - Toby's Choice

Death waited in the dark, just out of reach of the light. Toby's spirit sat looking at his body, dumped in Sherrin Woods by his abductor. A string of Japanese lanterns outlined a path; the spirit stood and wandered toward them. The laughter of children soon could be heard. There were growls and rustling in the shadows along the way, but Toby's heart stayed true.

He spotted light up ahead and soon stood at the edge of a clearing. The first thing that caught his eye was a three hundred foot Ferris wheel penetrating the skyline. He saw a Merry-Go-Round; a beautiful princess, with a ruby in her navel, handed him cotton candy as he walked by her concession. A man swallowed a sword that was in one hand, then removed it and swallowed fire from the end of a rod he held in his other hand. Calliope music bounced around children running toward a dunking ring. A man with a bowler hat and garters on the sleeves of his striped shirt held out three wooden rings for a chance to win if you could get a ring onto a metal milk bottle.

A woman in a bathing costume went by doing cartwheels to the amusement of children and concessionaires alike. And a woman on a low standing stage had her legs wrapped behind her head as she walked around on her hands. A man that stood nine feet tall walked in the other direction on legs that must have been twice Toby's height. His pants had wide stripes, and his top hat had a feather sticking out the side.

Toby watched a man with a top hat and tuxedo approaching. When he reached Toby, he bent at the waist and then stood, and handed Toby a ticket. "Use it any way you wish," he said, tipping his hat and then walking toward two clown acrobats, that thought they were a wheel racing around a pole.

The music seemed louder to Toby with a ticket in hand. Concession operators reached out to him, calling to him, arms outstretched. A heavily tattooed woman, wearing a boa constrictor for a necklace beckoned him with her fingertips.

Toby disposed of the paper cone that hosted the cotton candy. He turned in a circle and took in all the rides and attractions. There were short lines of children here and there; then he spotted a long line waiting for the Ferris wheel and ran towards it. He ran past the booth to win a goldfish, and a booth to knock over milk bottles. He saw a marksman testing her skills with a rifle, knocking down metal ducks with a BB gun – plink went the target, plink.

Once in line, Toby looked into the darkness, waiting his turn. The noises of the growls and rustlings in the shadows were drowned out by the sounds of popcorn popping, whistles blowing and clowns honking their horns.

The Ferris wheel started and stopped a few times, and then Toby was given a seat to himself. At first, the wheel moved slowly, as passengers boarded. Then it began to turn at just the right pace. Off to the south, Toby saw biplanes flying into and out of fluffy white clouds. They did somersaults and fancy twists and turns. The pilots waved when they saw Toby watching. There were wings of red, and yellow and green.

To the east, Toby could see an African savannah with wild beast roaming in the noonday sun. Gazelles dashed about, leaping tall and proud. A giant tortoise inched forward; the tortoise was in no particular hurry, and the anteater paid him no mind. A giraffe gazed back in his direction.

Looking west, Toby watched a pod of whales swimming peacefully, to their right, a group of dolphins accompanied them on this part of their journey. To the left a group of boys in colorful polyethylene kayaks, keeping pace. The Dolphins chattered as their voices joined with those of the whales as they released their songs to the sky and the sea. The newly born whales were at peace with their families and the earth.

Toby turned his attention north to the stars. They seemed close enough to reach. He turned and wiggled from beneath the bar across his lap. He stood on the seat of his gondola and climbed to his tiptoes with an outstretched arm. The galaxy was within his reach, as close as his jar of marbles, and held the same fascination. He beheld the red planet and tried to gather Saturn's rings. He was lost in space when the Ferris wheel moved, and toppled him out.

Captain Griffin Chaffey stood in the stalls and brushed Nuelle's coat and mane. He had stayed up late giving the carriage a good cleaning. With wheels greased, brass, polished and all the leather, freshly oiled, she could not be cleaner; she was a treat for the senses. It had that new carriage smell.

Nuelle received the best of treatment from Griffin. She knew that their passenger today must be very special, as he was taking extra care with every detail. She listened to him hum as he worked on her coat this morning. She drew energy from his energy.

At dusk they were ready, and the wheels rang louder and crisper along the cobblestoned streets on their route to pick up their fare. He pulled the carriage between the two gas street lamps and arrived just as they were lit from the end of a long pole designed for the purpose.

Griffin climbed down. He waved to the man who lit the lanterns. He took an apple from his pocket and shared it with Nuelle as they waited. At first, the stars arrived one by one, then handfuls, then a salt shaker of stars spilled across the night sky.

A path, lit by stardust, led Toby away from Sherrin Woods. Toby still clutched the ticket given to him by the ringmaster. He emerged from the woods; the starlit path led across a parkway. He could see a white carriage with a white mare waiting.

Emergency sirens broke the magic spell cast on the night. Toby pushed forward.

Griffin was at ease. He whispered to Nuelle when he saw Toby approach.

Toby strolled. He had a head full of visions, and not much wisdom, to filter what he had seen.

Griffin moved toward the step of the carriage. Toby arrived and looked up into Griffin's face.

A kaleidoscope of shapes and colors floated through his mind. He turned and pointed back toward the woods where a blue and red hue now filled the skyline above the trees as emergency vehicles gathered at the crime scene.

"Are you here for me?" Toby asked. "Where are you taking me?"

Griffin held out his hand. "Say hello to Nuelle. She is going to take you wherever you want to go." Griffin reached into the front seat and produced another apple. He cut it into pieces and handed two to Toby, "Feed one to Nuelle and have one yourself."

Toby did as requested. It was a thrill to have this beautiful beast take a part of an apple from his hand and nod in grateful appreciation.

Griffin led Toby back to the step and put his hand out.

Toby took it and climbed inside.

"There is a blanket for your legs underneath the seat if you need it. But it is a pleasant night; I don't think you are going to need it."

Once Toby was comfortable, Griffin climbed into the front seat and waited for Toby's choice.

The Carriage Driver[2] - Stone Angels

Lilith stepped from the doorway of the 'Gates of Hell' bar just in time to see The Carriage Driver turn down Summer Street. She was a prideful agent of darkness and felt she had a score to settle with this man and perhaps a chance for more. Her black heels tapped out messages of fear and anticipation following him, concealed in murky shadows.

Nuelle's ears twitched, and she turned her head this way and that, staring toward the edges of the gas lanterns reach. She carried unrest in her heart, as she moved towards home. Once there, she would be guided to park the carriage, and then the Captain would remove her harness and tack. Once in her stall she would be brushed and fed before the Captain took to his rest.

The routine was only broken this evening as Lilith watched; she stood, eyes flickering, as she contemplated her opportunity. A short man, dressed in black, carrying a silver-tipped cane climbed down from his small black carriage and walked to her side. His tail draped over his shoulder and held in place buttoned beneath an *epaulette. The liquid in the gutters near their feet began to bubble.* "Go bring others from nearby," she instructed.

Smoke rose from the concrete where she stood waiting. When five of the short men dressed in black, that guided the shuttles of doom arrived, she gave her instructions: tonight the fallen souls would just have to wait for their fate. She was going to steal the white horse that knew the way to the castle, and they were to delay The Carriage Driver.

When the damp fog of 2 a.m. rolled in she moved toward the stable where Nuelle slept. She swung the unlocked door wide and rushed toward the stall. Lilith was on Nuelle's back before she was fully awake. She rose high, but Lilith was muscular and determined.

The noise woke Griffin. A copy of William Morris' 'Defence of Guenevere' (1875) slid from his chest and hit the floor the same time as his feet. He found the light and his pants in a single movement and flew down the stairs to investigate.

Lilith held firm as Nuelle bolted from the stalls trying to rid herself of the rider. Heat from the rider's legs scorched her coat. Lilith's howling voice sent tremors of fear through Nuelle as she galloped into the devil's night.

As Griffin reached the bottom of the stairs, a black cane struck him behind one knee which toppled him. When he was standing again, an instant later, the small man was lifting it for another blow. Two others approached. Griffin jerked the first man, with one arm into the air, and threw him against the wall.

The black ball struck the wall and burst into a flurry of smoke and drifted back towards deep sorrow. Griffin watched for one second as two others took up the fight. A second blow and again a small man erupted into swirling smoke. The eerie scream of the descending reminded the others of what waited. They crouched and took choreographed steps backwards until they were outside and had room to run. They reached their carriages and hurried back into their obscurity.

Captain Chaffey got his boots, his coat, and hat. He grabbed a knapsack and went to the carriage and reached for the book. With the book secured, Griffith stepped through the door into the gusting torrent of piercing crisis. With tears, for Nuelle, in his eyes, he took two steps, stopped and went back into the house. In the kitchen, he found two apples and put them into the pocket of his coat. The cold night waited.

Within a block, he came on the two abandoned black carriages and two small black horses. He unhitched one, climbed on her back and rode toward the castle. He thought, even frightened that is where she would head.

Lilith with back arched shrieked with the madness of her triumph. That and Nuelle's hoofs hitting the cobblestoned path with fury sent alarms going in the castle. Four angels dispatched with urgency rushed to their emergency posts.

Swiping along the cobblestoned road, they spotted Lilith and recognized her as an agent of darkness, and they knew Nuelle by sight. One banked and turned back toward the castle. The other three flew past Nuelle and Lilith, landing on the pathway. They landed, spread their wings, and turned to stone, blocking any retreat.

Moments later, another group of angels flew to Nuelle's rescue, landing in front of Lilith's advance. They, too, landed and turned to stone. Stone angels snarled Lilith in her bid for heaven. She jumped from Nuelle's back. Nuelle's hair was charred, leaving Lilith's silhouette where she had straddled her.

As Griffin reached the spot from the South, a troop of angels arrived behind the row of stone angels from the North. Griffin stood on the back of his small black mount to climb over the stone barricade.

He and Nuelle now faced Lilith. She looked to the path forward and back. She thought if she could reach the small black horse, she might live to try another day. She gauged her chances. Lilith knew she had weakened Nuelle. She felt the Captain would not be thinking straight.

The troop of angels made any chance for the castle fruitless. She swallowed hard and leapt over the short railing. The Captain and Nuelle went to the rail and watched her fall.

As the stone angels returned to their more nimble selves, the black horse turned and fled. The group of angels that protected the castle swarmed around the Captain and Nuelle. They all returned to the castle.

In the morning, Griffin was in a stall with Nuelle, brushing her hair. He had clipped as much of the charred hair as possible, and now they would just have to wait for it to grow out. They were interrupted as the tall man in a tuxedo entered.

"I have been told to deliver a message," he began with sadness in his eyes. "I have been chosen to tell you that you cannot go back to your home and carriage. You are invited to stay here. Or of course, you can select any destination." He made a gesture with his arms, of exasperation. "Word from higher up is that the agent of darkness will stalk you and try to use you for another attempt to breach, through guile or deceit her irrevocable contract earned through her actions during her life." He moved closer, "I heard in the kitchen that a dozen angels would volunteer to follow you anywhere of your choosing."

Griffin knew the man was not finished and was unhappy with the pause.

"There is one last thing," he reached out his arm, "they have asked that you surrender the Book."

Nuelle swished her white tail and tossed her magnificent white mane. Griffin looked around. Reaching into a pocket, he retrieved an apple. He cut the apple into four pieces and offered one piece to the man in the tuxedo. When declined, Griffin fed two pieces to Nuelle and ate the others.

"Who is going to take my place?" Griffin asked, looking around for his knapsack. He spotted it and walked to it. He reached inside and opened the book to the last page. There was the name of a man who was due to be picked up hours ago. He slapped the book closed. "I guess he will just have to wait."

Griffin led Nuelle out of the stable where they had spent the early morning hours. He took a hold of a handful of mane and began to walk off past the castle, down the cobblestone pathway.

The man in the tuxedo rushed out the door and called out, "There may be an opening in the South."

Walking to Goleta

This is not part of The Carriage Driver Series
I have added it here to preserve it.

It was one of those deceptive California winter days, the afternoon temperature hovered around sixty-five degrees. Tom sat in the crook of the root of the old oak tree and its trunk looking out over the Pacific. The Santa Barbara morning fog had burned off. A scarf of orange California poppy ran up along the bank toward the two-lane asphalt road above.

Tom sat and thought about the age of the tree he now called his home. The folded up Dear John letter and his military exit DD-214 form were in his otherwise empty wallet. The letter explained that his kid brother had fallen in love, with his sweetheart. They had married before Tom was shipped home from his campaigns in Sicily. When mustered out of the Army he returned to the States but never returned home. He headed west and had gone as far west as the continent would allow. The easiest thing to think about was the age of this tree.

There were orange orchards about a mile south of where he sat, and his friend Damian had gone hunting for the earth's bounty. Damian needed to be beneath trees that were not exploding from daily German ordinance and walking in fields not secured by enemy crossfire. In the distance, Tom saw a small dot and he thought it might be Damian returning with his jacket pockets bulging with Navel Oranges for their afternoon meal.

The long sprawling branches of the oak provided deep shade and even some protection from the rare rainfall. A canal rushing off to the ocean gave them access to fresh, clean water. This was a quiet place on this earth. Everything seemed quiet after Sicily for Tom and Damian mostly survived the cold hell offered by the Ardennes, but only mostly. There was still the occasional midnight screaming as one of the three veterans woke from a visit from their past.

Donnie had his own way about him. He had sandy blonde hair and a movie star smile. His calm was deceptive. His time at war was spent in the Pacific. Every morning he returned to the beach, he needed to push footsteps of sand atop his Pacific memories. Anytime there was a conversation about his time in the war, he just looked at the ground and shook his head.

Tom had lived under the tree now for going on one year. One day, many months back Damian showed up and tossed Tom two oranges taken from his oversize coat pockets and he never left. Shortly after that Tom and Damian found Donnie drunk on the side of the road just above them on the highway. They each threw one of his arms over their shoulders and dragged him beneath the oak. The toes of his shoes left a trail in the dirt to the oak tree. Twenty-four hours later he woke, said "Hello" and had also never left.

The men bathed in the ocean and rinsed in the fresh water of the stream. Their military experience taught them how to get by and keep clean. If they needed money one or all would walk into the sleepy town and find some day labor. It was an agricultural area and there was plenty. If you were paying attention, you would hear the mission bells toll at noon.

There were wine vineyards just to the east above the mission. Orange and lemon groves were to the south, extending miles and there were even some stands of grapefruit trees. The men had laid down their responsibilities of war and determined not to be in a hurry.

Tom watched Damian for a moment, then went back to thinking about the tree. He guessed it was planted sometime in the 1600's. The local history told him the Chumash Indians were in this area then, even before the Spanish. Even before the mission. The fresh salt air slowly did its work to heal him.

Donnie left deep footprints in the sand as he walked away from the Pacific, back up toward the tree. His blonde hair flew in all directions. He wore khaki pants, no belt, pant legs rolled up to his calves. In one hand, he carried a fishing pole that someone had 'forgotten' along the beach and in his other hand he held two bonitos and a small sack with mussels. He occasionally caught a mackerel, but not today.

Tom grunted as he pushed himself to stand. He gathered up some twigs and began to prepare a fire. They were going to eat well tonight. Damian arrived with a big smile on his face. He dumped a dozen Navel oranges on the ground near the fire pit ring of rocks.

Tom picked up the first bonito and gutted it with a small sharp knife he wore in a sheath on his belt. In no time, the two fish were frying, covered with orange peel and a dash of lemon. The men took their third of the fish and the oranges. There was only water with this meal. But the men had their fill. The wine would have to wait.

After their meal, Tom cleaned up. He gathered the entrails and tossed them into an empty Bush's Pork & Beans tin can. Donnie would use it for crab bait along the rough sea wall. When the chores were done, he sat back down, he was now cradled safely in the crook of the arm of the old oak and stared out at the full moon that lay on the horizon at the rim of the world. He patted his shirt pocket out of habit for a pack of smokes, but there were none among them.

Tom, Damian now dressed in three layers curled up near the trunk of the oak. Donnie went into the tree and found his place, the collar of his old field jacket pulled up around his neck. In the Pacific, he learned to sleep in a tree. Donnie had been with them two months before he had mentioned being on Tarawa.

The flames of the campfire sputtered to a glowing pile of amber. The chatter of the sandpipers drew to a close. The three men slept in safety beneath the centuries-old oak.

The men awoke to the sound of the surf, and seabirds which slowly was driving out the sounds of cannon. The rays of the sun delivered the citrus scent of dawn. Donnie climbed down from the tree and grabbed the tin of entrails and walked toward the rugged rocks on the edge of the world where he felt most comfortable. It also would provide the men their dinner. The Sanderlings greeted him, almost as one of their own. Tom stood and stretched. He promised to do some kitchen duty at the local café and would have to hustle to get an egg and coffee, from the Mexican cook before the duty he started, that of cleaning the pots and pans and mopping the place out before they opened. Damian headed off towards Mrs. Patterson's place, he often borrowed her boy's 22 caliber rifle and walked off into the foothills with the understanding that the first rabbit belonged to the Patterson's pot.

As the sun began to set, Donnie had two eating size crabs, and a halibut that had got himself caught at low tide in the recessed crevices in the rocks. Damian had pockets full of oranges and a nice plump rabbit. Tom brought back a pack of cigarettes, and he was paid two extra eggs for dragging some old crates back up to a farm on the poor side of town.

It was a good day for them all. The fire again moved toward amber and the men sat back and each smoked their cigarette. The rabbit and crab were now just a pleasant memory. Donnie went to the spring and washed out his shirt and returned and hung it to dry. He put on his field jacket and zipped it tight at the neck. He climbed into his place in the tree and fell asleep. The other two men drifted off to sleep in the embrace and safety of moonlight.

Donnie's feet hit the dirt with the quiet a panther would be proud of as he woke to the sound of a vehicle's wheels slowly making their way down the path that marked his own arrival. Tom's eyes opened, he remained completely still, sensing an unspoken danger. The car's headlights arched across the scene. Tom stood in time to see Damian slip away into the brush like a boa constrictor.

The Sheriff's car stopped about ten yards in front of Tom. With the lights still on, the Sheriff Deputy climbed out of the car and walked to the front of his car. The deputy was about twenty-five years old. "Call your friends out of the bushes," he called to Tom. "The one that crawled away," he pointed, "over there somewhere." He continued, "I saw the burning embers and wanted to make sure the whole town was not in jeopardy."

Damian hearing this stepped from the shadows just a few feet from where the deputy stood. Donnie followed suit, he cleared his throat, causing the deputy to turn to his right to see just who was standing so close to him. The Deputy had spent the war years in and around the Philippines; a man in the shadows was not going to shake him.

A quick survey of the men told the Deputy these were men and men he felt comfortable with. He was familiar with the look in their eyes. That stare that looked past what was in front of them to some horror they had to resolve. He walked towards Tom and reaching him put his hand out. He said, "Philippines."

Tom replied, "Sicily," and pointing at Damian he said, "Belgium and Germany," then pointing at Donnie he said, "Marine on Tarawa. I am Tom; you likely have seen me in town. That is Damian and Donnie."

"I'm Alfonso, but I am mostly called Deputy." He turned and walked to the trunk of his car. He reached into a box of food earmarked for charity and grabbed two cans of beans. We walked back towards Tom and handed them to him. "As long as I don't get any complaints, I don't have to do anything about you," he turned, went back to his car and backed up the hill to the highway spreading dust as he went.

The night settled back down. Each man felt they had been put on notice. Tom shifted down in his space and listened to the ocean carry him away. Damian after a day in the foothills fell into a deep sleep and Donnie had just begun to let himself sleep when he heard a car stop on the highway. Then a moment later he heard a car door slam shut and the wheels bit the dust as the car pulled away rapidly.

Donnie silently dropped to the ground. He could hear something up on the highway. The other men slept, his footsteps made no sound as he climbed up the path back to the roadside. It was dark; he pulled a match from his pocket and lit it. In the darkness, it seemed like a flare. His eye caught the movement at the same time the match burnt his finger. He put his finger in his mouth for a second and then lit another. He moved close to what looked like something wrapped in an old piece of blanket. The something moved. He tapped the bundle with the toe of his shoe and the bundle cried. Quickly he bent down and loosened the tucked in swathe.

The boy with cinnamon skin broke into a smile that covered his face. Donnie picked him and the blanket up and walked back toward the oak.

His arrival woke Tom. To himself he wondered how Donnie could get out of the tree without him becoming alert. "What do you have there?" Tom asked with genuine curiosity.

"Another brother." He handed Tom, the baby.

Tom looked up the hill. He looked at Donnie and asked the obvious question. "Where did you get him?" He wanted to hand him back.

Damian woke and sat up, "What are you guys doing?" He rubbed his eyes and stood up to see what Tom was holding. When he saw, he said, "What are you guys doing with a baby? Are you crazy? Donnie?"

"Someone dumped him on the side of the road. Kind of like us if you think about it." Donnie offered.

Tom was tired of holding him. "Here, you hold him." He handed the baby to Damian and went to his duffle bag. He found a cord and took a pair of pants and in no time had made a makeshift hammock that hung close to the ground. He took the baby from Damian and put him in the makeshift swing and gave the bundle a push and let it gently sway. He gave Donnie a look like this was all his fault. Still looking at Donnie, he said, "You have anything like a sweater?"

Damian found a long johns shirt in his kit and handed it to Tom, who draped it around the baby who had already fallen asleep. "He's asleep. Maybe we should get some sleep."

Donnie lay on the ground near the swaying hammock. They all slept.

Damian was the last one to wake up in the morning. Tom slipped off early into town to find work, and Donnie went to the shore to gather food for dinner. Damian looked over at the still hammock. The baby was still there and smiling. Damian went over and looked at this new addition. "Come on," he said and picked him up. He walked over to the stream cleaned off his long john shirt and the baby and himself, then walked back. He hung the wet shirt up to dry in the cold morning air and took his last semi-clean undershirt shirt and slipped it over the baby.

He sat down and emptied his kit in front of him. He tossed his finger through his belongings. He was wearing most of what he owned. There were belts and a razor and some clean socks. The baby wore the only clean undershirt he owned. There were a couple of Army issue handkerchiefs. Damian stared. He picked up the bag. It had a shoulder strap, sturdy stitching and a drawstring at the top. He grabbed some sticks from the kindling pile and broke them to the length he thought he would need when he had four of them, he flipped the bag over, turned up all the edges put a thick twig on each side and rolled them several times over. He then flipped the bag back over and had a pouch of sorts with a strap. He put the baby in the new cradle. He cut a hole in the bag near the baby's feet, then slipped a hankie through and tied a loop. He put the strap around his neck and clipped the clasp to the new cloth loop. With his new rig, he walked off towards the orange groves vowing not to be the last one awake in the morning.

Near dusk, Damian and Tom headed back toward the oak. Tom was proud; he found some work and had brought home cans of milk and some cloth, taken from the charity stores bins out in front. Donnie had fish stew cooking. Damian had pockets full of walnuts and oranges. Tom took the baby and set him on the ground and rigged the hammock again. Then he put a tin of water on the coals to warm. With some effort, the baby was cleaned and covered enough to keep him comfortable and put back swinging in the hammock.

When Tom returned from cleaning everything the baby touched he found Damian dripping milk into the baby's mouth from a straw that Tom thought to bring.

"You did good today Tom," Damian said. "The milk is a perfect idea. Once we open a can, it is not going to be fit to drink for very long."

"I'll get some more," Tom told them.

"We can't keep him," Donnie uncharacteristically added his two-cents worth. "We have to think of what to do."

"We could find the Deputy. He would know something." Damian pushed dirt with his foot at the thought.

"The kid would end up in some damn institution. I don't want that for him." Tom had begun feeling paternal. "Ok, let's agree to think about the solution. The three of us should be able to take care of him while we do that. You all agree?" It was the first call for a vote in all the time they had been sheltered by the oak.

A week had passed. Tom would go into town each morning. He began to notice tinsel and pine wreaths. Signs of Christmas appeared with strings of light and bells. He had grown up with real winters on the east coast. Here you had to be reminded that it was winter. He began to learn each shopkeeper's name as he found work, sweeping or painting or repairing. That evening he brought back food for the baby and something warm.

Damian did most of the watching out for the baby during the day. Tom found a long woolen scarf that made a better sling for the baby to ride in as Damian roamed the orchards and fields. When Damian wanted to hunt, Donnie watched the baby as the crying alerted the rabbits.

Each night the men talked about the solutions to a home for the baby, but had not come up with anything agreeable. Until Saturday night after dinner Damian announced he wanted the other two to go with him in the morning. He wanted to show them something.

In the morning with no explanation, the men followed Damian. It was a long walk through the orchards at first, and then Damian led them to a cemetery. Donnie and Tom exchanged glances. Damian saw them, but did not say anything. He walked through some rows and then stopped. He pointed to a stone marker that read: Baby Hernandez, December 25, 1945, 8 a.m. to midnight.

"Do you think we can find the parents?" Tom asked.

Donnie was all ears.

"I found them. The Patterson's know the family, and Mrs. Patterson told me where they are. They don't live too far from here at the edge of Goleta," Damian said to his friends.

"Can I hold him?" Donnie asked, realizing what was happening.

Damian lifted the sling over his head and handed the bundle to Donnie. Donnie put the knot behind his neck, and the baby rested against his chest. The three men turned and walked toward the sunset back to the oak.

"When should we do it?" Tom asked. "We are going to have to go into town and gather some things first."

"What things?" Damian asked.

"A basket and some clean clothes and maybe a box of food and a new blanket. I have done so much work this week that I have the money," Tom offered.

"Christmas is in two days. I think we should drop him off on Christmas Eve." Damian was feeling pride.

"If we are going to eat tonight, we had better get busy." Donnie turned, made an adjustment to the sling and began back.

"Maybe we can walk through town and start picking up some things," Tom suggested.

Two days before Christmas and the town lit up. Red and green tinsel everywhere. The smell of fresh pine wreaths was comforting. The smell of spice apple pie filled the air. Tom suggested that they stop in and indulge in a slice of apple pie at the local café.

The men entered and ordered pie and coffee. The waitress was so curious, but said nothing to the men. They ate and paid their bill and left. It was then that the waitress called for the Deputy. She could not help herself but to report these three coarse looking men and one was carrying a baby.

Tom, Damian, and Donnie found a reed basket at the charity shop and a colorful blanket. They went to the grocers and bought canned milk and two jars of baby food. The men had not thought about the war for days.

Deputy Alfonso was unhappy at the complaint about three rough looking men with an infant. It could be three different men just passing through, but he would have to check. He knew what these men had gone through like so many others. He thought of how easily he could have become one of them. He drove to the Oak where he knew they lived and found the place empty, but not deserted so he left.

As the men reached the camp, it was Donnie, who said, "Someone has been here. Those are fresh tire tracks."

"As far as I know only that Sheriff knows we were here," Tom told him.

"We don't dare stay here," Damian said. "It would be that Deputy's duty to take the boy from us."

Donnie grabbed the things that were hanging to dry and stuffed them in his bag. He took his fishing pole and planned to return it near where he found it. He intended to make sure the areas he fished and hunted crab were back to where no one would ever know he was there.

Tom packed his kit and waited. Damian did not have much of a kit. Just pockets full of oranges. In an hour, the men stood and looked over the area under the safety of the oak that had been home for this part of their life. Tom would miss the place the most. He had been here the longest.

Tom with the baby suspended from his neck and his duffle bag over his shoulder, walked up the steep path to the highway. Damian hoisted his bag over his shoulder and the box of food under his arm and followed. Donnie with his change of clothes tied in a bundle in one hand and the basket in the other looked around one last time and walked as quietly as a panther up the slope. At the highway, Damian and Donnie each took a side of Tom and they walked in the darkness towards Goleta. They spent the night and the day in the foothills and waited.

Now, it was the 24th of December. They waited in the foothills along this stretch out of sight of the highway and waited for nightfall. They did not light a fire. Damian pulled oranges from his deep coat pockets, and also tossed each of the men some walnuts. They planned to wait until the Hernandez household quieted down and the lights were turned off to make their delivery. The men took turns holding the baby and saying their goodbyes.

When Tom guessed it was about 9 p.m. he stood up. The three walked to the Hernandez house, just a small square of a place with dirt for a yard and a low fence made from twigs and branches and an arched entry. They made a sad silhouette.

Tom took the sling from around his neck and handed the baby to Donnie. Donnie had found the baby and the men thought it fair that he leave the baby. Tom took his last two cigarettes from the package and tore the paper, on the inside non-printed side, he wrote the words, 'Baby Hernandez' and tucked the printed words in the blanket with the baby.

Donnie took the sling and untied the knot. He made a pad and stuffed it into the basket and put the baby into it. He put the new blanket over him and tucked it in. Donnie with the basket and Damian with the box of food walked to the front door and put their packages down. Damian ran back to the shadows and when he saw both men were clear, he knocked on the door and ran toward the archway.

The three men thought they were wise, but eight-year-old Margareta was keeping a sharp eye out for Santa Claus and saw their silhouettes.

Mr. Hernandez turned on the porch light, opened the door and looked down at the basket. He was bending over to pick the basket up when his wife arrived at the door wearing her nightgown. She saw the baby and had him in her arms before her husband who then lifted the small box of food. He looked around, but saw nothing and closed the door behind him.

In a moment, all the lights in the house were on. Santa Claus had arrived early.

Donnie could hear the woman crying. It reminded him of his mother and tears formed in his eyes. The first tears he allowed himself in five years.

The men walked back to the highway. There were miles to go before reaching Goleta where they hoped they could catch a bus. The North Star visible in the sky above them, helped to light the way. They were a mile away from the Hernandez house when the Sheriff Deputy's car pulled up behind them on the highway lights flashing.

Deputy Alfonso parked as far off the road as possible and got out. "I heard one of you had a baby. Any truth to that?"

"Officer, we don't have a baby. We just thought we would try someplace new." Tom was the spokesperson.

"Can I check your bags?" Deputy Alfonso asked.

Tom and Damian unslung their bags and tossed them on the ground. Donnie threw his change of close wrapped in his extra shirt on the ground. Deputy Alfonso did not make a move for them, none of these men would throw a baby on the ground, he was sure of that.

"Where're you fellows going at this hour?" Alfonso asked.

"We are hoping there is a bus station in Goleta," Tom told him. He liked Alfonso.

"That's four miles. If you want, you can hop in the back and I'll give you a lift."

The men climbed in, no sense walking four miles if you can ride.

Deputy Alfonso dropped them at the door of the station. He told them it was likely closed until the day after Christmas, but the buses still came and if you could pay the driver, they would let you in. The men thanked him and said goodbye.

An hour later a bus came heading south toward Los Angeles. Tom paid the fare for Donnie, who said he had heard of a place called Malibu and that is where he was heading to make a new life.

Around two a.m. a bus slowed and asked where they were headed. Damian was heading north. He talked to someone once that told him about a place called Moss Landing an artist colony and he thought he would fit in there. Tom paid his fare and shook his hand and watched the bus until it disappeared into the darkness.

He sat on his duffle bag. He pulled the wallet out of his pocket that held the DD-214, the Dear John letter, and three twenty dollar bills. He opened the letter and read it one more time. He stared at it a long time, then tore it into little pieces and let the pieces be tumbled away by the breeze.

The next bus came by on Christmas morning. It slowed and stopped, a young pregnant couple in love got off smiling. "Where you headed?" called the driver. He looked at Tom's eyes and said, "I'm William, North Africa."

"Tom, Sicily." Tom smiled and said, "East. I am going home."

"All the eastbound buses leave out of Los Angeles, climb on, I'll get you as far as Ventura."

Tom climbed aboard and started to hand the driver money, but was waved off; he took a seat. In just a few miles, they were driving through Santa Barbara and passed the centuries-old oak. Tom leaned back and sunk into the seat; the bus rolled along through Montecito, and Summerland and Carpentaria; as the sun rose higher he began to wonder just who had saved who. He stared out the window as the panorama of La Conchita and Mussel Shoals receded into the past. Tom - Sicily closed his eyes the bells of his missions silenced.

Acknowledgement

I met Maria Jordan at Emerald Wells Café. She is funny, witty and added warmth to the atmosphere. She is a writer with a reassuring voice. Her work has been compiled into an anthology titled *The Rain and Everything* and her children's book *Kylie's Blossoms* is a bouquet to savor. She is a natural storyteller. She shares her life experiences and the people that she has met in her nursing career with us with heartfelt charm. Throughout her stories one thing becomes clear, she loves people, all sizes, and shapes and with an abundance of compassion she assists them. She has risen above life's adversities and kept her principles intact. Her latest passion as a professor of nursing studies is flourishing.

She has offered to write an introduction to each of my self-published books. That is a sure sign of her generosity.

Acknowledgement

Genna Eastman is a professional consultant and author. She writes under the pseudonym, Genna East, for the website, Hubpages. It is a privilege to count Genna among my friends. Her writing is crafted with the utmost of care, and the subtle nature of her words draws her readers into many an enchanting journey. Her every written word seems well chosen and when a story of hers is finished, the results are often a sculpted piece of art. She does not mind leading her readers into dark situations, but she always hands them a candle to find their way. Much of her work is available to read at no charge on Hubpages. If you are an avid reader of short stories and enjoy intricate poetry, treat yourself to a treasure chest of the written word. Be intrigued by *The Pandion Prophecy,* delighted by *Bessie*, swept away along *The Forgotten Roads of Ancient Rome*, and have your spirit lifted with *Daniel of Lucid Dreams* – a poem.

From the same author

Braids – Angel's Field

Angel is the caretaker of a way station to heaven. The guardians that prepare the girls for their final journey live in the trees of the nearby peach orchard. Everything is peaceful until a girl named Hope is found stranded at Angel's Field because her guardian has been abducted. It is up to Angel and Cyrus a woodsmen and keeper of the orchard to recover her. Joined by Carpenter from a way station for young boys called 'The Swing Zone', the three leave their peaceful valley and set off towards the river.

Captain Castel, whose daughter is very ill, is the caretaker of another way station for people going in the opposite direction across the river. Once the toll is paid, there is no return. A thief named Messr. See de Arogänt, called Seede who operates a peddler's wagon is hired by Captain Castel to bring him a guardian.

Angel, Cyrus, and Carpenter find themselves on a mission to sustain Hope.

When a rumor reaches the ears of Captain Castel that a guardian may be acquired that could save his sick daughter he sets his plan in motion. A thief named Messr. See de Arogänt, called Seede who operates a peddler's wagon is hired by Captain Castel to bring him a guardian. All appears to be going well for Seede and Captain Castel when they are found out.

A little girl is left behind in Angel's Field because her guardian has been abducted. It is up to Angel and Cyrus a woodsmen and keeper of the orchard to recover her. Joined by Carpenter from a way station for young boys called 'The Swing Zone', the three leave their peaceful valley and set off towards the river.

Cyrus and Angel have lived a peaceful existence in their valley as caretakers of Angel's Field, a way station for young girls on their journey to heaven. Join Angel, Cyrus, and Carpenter as they make their way down the mountain and across the river in pursuit of the girl named Hope's guardian angel.

Emerald Wells Café and Pear Blossom Lane

People ask me where I am from. Since I was a Marine Corp brat, I tell them I am not from anywhere. If I could be from somewhere it, would be a place like Emerald Wells,Texas, just off the crossroads. Here you will find Earl in the kitchen of Emerald Wells Café. The owner's name is Emerald Wells, called Em by everyone in town. She does the waitressing.

Carl from Carl's Automotive stops in for breakfast every morning to say 'Hey.' He sits on the stool at the end of the counter. He likes that Em pats his shoulder the first time she passes by. He also likes to watch Gabby the owner of Let's Dress Up as she rushes across the street from her shop to the Café for her morning coffee and whatever looks good in the glass-domed dessert tray.

The Café is the center of the world for Earl, Em, Carl, Dale the Sheriff, who has known them all for their entire lives. The cast also include the Townsends whose place is out on the highway where they tend their orchards and Tom who is retired and bought the empty gas station at the turnoff to Emerald Wells and converted it first to his abode, then The Trading Post.

The group meets monthly and shares their writing in the form of poetry readings. They call the event, Speakeasy Night. They put on their go to meeting clothes, share their poetry, eat desserts and have a good time drinking special tea out of Em's Mom's china cups.

Earl, Carl, and Jimmy served as Marines in Korea. Jimmy did not come home; Army Captain Harold Tomlin was one second late arriving in his tank to save him. Harold shows up in Emerald Wells and is so taken with Em that a courtship begins.

What genre do you ask? It's a western. It's a poetry book. It's a romance. It's a food book. It's the lost biography of the USA. In my heart, I am from Emerald Wells.

The Quinn Moosebroker Mysteries

Detective Quinn Moosebroker arrived in the sleepy town of Clearview Terrace a broken man. A shootout in the line of duty killed his partner and a second bullet ended his career with the Allentown Police Department. In his forced retirement, he lives with his daughter Kate and has become a Sunday painter. His one activity is the restoration of a 1946 wood-paneled Chrysler Town and Country and an occasional trip to the local used book shop run by Blake Knightly.

Kate sets her father up on a blind date with the widow Betty Atwood to see a local play at a community theater. At the end of act one Pepper Bishop, owner of the Second Street Mystery Playhouse is murdered.

Betty Atwood starts the beginning of the best first date in history and the best thing that has happened to her in the years since her husband's passing. The couples, casual encounter quickly develops into a partnership that unveils a pornographer's scheme to sell photographs of non-consenting Clearview Terrace ladies to a big city true-detective publisher.

During Quinn and Betty's investigation Quinn bumps heads with the local authority in the form of Detective DeLaMonte, a renegade dismissed from the New Orleans Police Department.

Eleanor Pennyworth finds Quinn Moosebroker's name in an address book with the word 'trusted' written in pencil. When her partner is found dead in his Clearview Terrace home, she calls in Quinn to investigate a missing literary manuscript known as *Night of the Falling.* Quinn and Betty find themselves in a world of book people and rare book treasures.

Quinn relays a conversation about a young man's dream of murder to Betty he overheard on a quiet Saturday afternoon at the local barbershop. The story hits Betty so hard that while she tried to sleep that night she received a visitor in the form of a little boy at the foot of her bed. The haunting guest and Quinn's growing loyalty to Betty lead them to a government cover-up at a North Carolina Marine Corp Camp and to an aging Marine and his estranged wife.

On the return home, along a cold, dark southern highway, Betty adjusts the Town and Country's radio and a broadcast that correctly describes the night he was shot and his partner was killed sends them on a detour deep into a steel town and Quinn's past. The investigation undoes Dolan Ó Braonáin a local crime boss and exposes the far-reaching tentacles of his organization.

An innocent trip to the grand opening of a Clearview Terrace thrift store and an unexpected find send this detective duo skirting along the edges of stolen Nazi loot as they do their best to find the rightful owner of a piece of art that has survived all that has come its way.

Clearview Terrace will never be the same.

The Carriage Driver (one)

We are all led to believe that there is life after death. Western religion in all of its forms advises us so. Eastern religions have their own versions and many promises are made in these religions as well. No matter the religion or continent of the world, promises have been made.

The *hereafter* or *afterlife* holds many mysteries for all of us. There does not seem to be any clear measure of what lies ahead. This work presents the instances where a person's life has led to a promised land.

We are all familiar with images of the boatman in a dark pool with a shrouded body with its eyes covered with coins, carrying a soul to the land of the dead. The skiff glides into a murky gloom and drifts silently into the unknown that waits across the river Styx.

The Carriage Driver requires no money; he waits patiently for all those that have gained admittance to the next higher life. The concept is simplicity itself. The Carriage Driver with his beautiful and intuitive white mare Nuelle provides passage. If the passenger wishes to wait for a loved one, there is a castle in the sky whose spires puncture heaven to accommodate them.

Those that have avoided the gates of hell have obviously gained special privilege. These stories explore those privileges. The old man and the stillborn child decide to return as twin brothers. The homeless woman decides to wait at the castle for her son's turn before they continue on. When it is the turn of a husband and wife of half a century who were born the same day, hour, and minute to go, they choose to ride the back of a whale with Ursa Major as their guide to the heavens.

The setting is Boston, with all of its history. But there are Carriage Drivers in all cities, towns, boroughs and villages. These stories bring us hope, they inspire what is good in us and they are meant to make you think about the setting of your hereafter. Take pause, Nuelle and The Carriage Driver are waiting for you and your loved ones.

I recommend

Maria Jordan's, ***The Rain and Everything***

'The Rain and Everything' is at once a tribute, an affirmation, and a guide. The stories will reach inside you where you live. The writer's experiences are rich and her wisdom is strong. She shares her foundation stone and the secret of her inner strength, learned at her mother's knee.

Along the way, poetry will encourage you to face life's adversities with courage. Some words trickle as soft as rain and others crackle like thunder. The style will carry you along as she relays the stories of heroes both big and small, two footed and four-footed, that she met along the way.

The wisdom of her words forms an ellipse through both the practical and the clinically mad. Her nursing career brought her face to face with the homeless and the homicidal. You will cheer her perseverance and shed tears at the injustices she encountered.

This is a volume that you will reach for often. You will ponder and you will appreciate what is good in your world. Roll up your shirtsleeves, pour yourself a cold drink and dive in. Reading Maria Jordan is like skipping stones across a lake on a summer day. There is love and affirmation to be found between these covers.

Kimmie Thompson's, ***Within My Heart***

This book is a collection of short stories and poems that I have written over the last few years. My heart's desire is that they will bless you, place a smile upon your face, but most of all inspire you. Some are fiction and some are non-fiction, each carrying a special message from the depths of my heart.

Within my heart,

Lies an ocean of lost dreams,

They wait in silence.

A buried treasure,

Waiting to be discovered,

That will set my heart free.

Find these fine titles on Amazon.com

www.ingramcontent.com/pod-product-compliance
Lightning Source LLC
LaVergne TN
LVHW010918110826
845149LV00013B/2420